MAMA SAVES A VICTIM

A NEW HOLLOWAY HOUSE MYSTERY

BY

Nora DeLoach

Holloway House Publishing Company
Los Angeles, California

Holloway House Books by Nora DeLoach

Silas
Mama Solves A Murder
Mama Traps A Killer
Mama Stands Accused
Mama Saves A Victim

An Original Holloway House Edition

Printed in the United States of America

ISBN O-87067-874-4
First Holloway House Edition: June 1997

MAMA SAVES
A VICTIM

Dedicated to My Mother

Agatha Marcelle Frazier

CHAPTER ONE

I opened my eyes. The only light in the room came from the digital alarm clock, a pale green glow floating across the night table and settling onto the telephone. I lay huddled beneath my comforter, trying to keep a feeling of panic at bay, with a sense of an impending disaster lurking in the background.

I pulled the comforter to my chin. Cliff, my boyfriend, had surprised me when he called a few nights ago saying that he had to fly to Los Angeles. It was his third trip out of town in less than a month. He offered no apology nor words of regret; he simply said that he had to go.

I cringed. Another weekend alone in Atlanta. Cliff's chocolate complexion and short haircut reminded me of Richard Roundtree. What had started out as an attraction had grown into more, something much more. We were partners, I'd decided, partners for life. My brow lifted. I wondered whether I was naive to think that Cliff felt the same way.

I was trying to deal with my doubts when the phone rang. I picked it up, expecting Cliff's voice.

It was Mama. Her tone cut through my feelings. "Hester and Fingers visited last night," she said.

I hope that there are few families with a member like Mama's third cousin's son. We call him Fingers because he takes things that don't belong to him. He's thirteen, but we've known of his habit since he was six. Fingers keeps what he takes until you ask for it, then he swears that he doesn't remember taking it. Everybody except his mother doubts his memory.

I looked at the clock; it was 6:00 a.m. "What are you missing?" I asked.

"A silver music box I bought when your father was stationed in Germany."

"When are you going to go get it back?" I asked.

"Tomorrow," she said. "Want to go with me?"

"Y-yeah," I stuttered. "Cliff's out of town."

"He's gone again?" she said. "When will he get back?"

"Tuesday."

"He's been going out of town a lot lately, hasn't he?"

I stiffened; I didn't answer her question.

"What time will you be here?" She asked.

"I'll pack a bag and leave straight from work." I paused. "I won't stop to eat so I should get to Otis around ten-thirty."

The afternoon sky was dark. Night fell a little after 6:00 p.m. just as I pulled onto I-20 East. The heavy blackness that quickly engulfed North Georgia wasn't helping my nerves.

The next morning, the skies were still heavy and a steady drizzle was falling. I spent the first part of the day trying to decide whether I was stupidly loyal or rightfully suspicious of Cliff's frequent business trips. I didn't mention it to Mama because I thought she would encourage my uncertainty.

Around two o'clock, Mama and I were driving back to Otis from Sandford where we'd visited her cousin Hester. The rain and the clouds caused the trees to cast threatening shadows.

My Mama's name is Grace but she's called Candi because of her complexion. It's like candied sweet potatoes. Mama is the one black woman who could be a bona fide spokeswoman for the Dove soap commercial. She had recovered her music box. "You know, I'm beginning to believe that Fingers doesn't remember taking things."

We were approaching the Oaktree Crossing when I glanced at the box in my mother's hand. I looked for a second, then turned to see a young woman dart out in front of my car. I slammed on the brakes, turned the wheel, but it was too late. I hit her! The car skidded to a stop; we jumped out.

The woman's eyes were closed. Blood, with its pungent scent, oozed from her flesh. She came awake with a jerk, winded and coughing. Mama was on her knees. "Baby, don't move," Mama said, her oval eyes warm and compassionate. "Simone," she ordered, "call an ambulance!"

I rushed to make the call on my car phone. When I got back, Mama glanced at me, then she stood up. At first, Mama hesitated as if she considered something for a second but then put it aside. "Child, you're getting soaking wet," Mama said, walking back toward the car.

The young woman's eyes darkened. Although her complexion was milky white, she had features that screamed black blood ran through her veins. She was a red-bone, or what locals called an Ascian. When she pulled me to her, I got a feeling that I'd seen her before. "This ain't nothing like what's going to happen to me if I don't get away from this place!" she said, her voice trembling.

From somewhere, I smelled a strange pungent odor that reminded me of something, I realized, I didn't want to remember. Then, for the first time, I saw it—the face of a man. His cheeks were boney, his eyes piercing. I blinked. A twinge of nausea wrenched my stomach. In a moment, the face disappeared. I was looking in the girl's eyes. She squeezed my arm. "Listen," she said, "give me a break, let me get away."

I shook my arm free. "Once we get you to the hospital..."

The young lady interrupted. "No hospital!" she snapped. She struggled but she was obviously in pain. And deeply frightened.

I heard the approaching ambulance. Mama walked toward us, a jacket thrown across her arm, an umbrella over her head. The young woman leaned back. "I don't need no hospital!" she said again.

Paramedics jumped out and took over. A few minutes later they were sliding her inside the back of the ambulance. Mama threw the jacket over my shoulders and I turned to see her greet Rick Martin, the sheriff's deputy. He had heard the ambulance call. Mama told him that the woman appeared like a ghost in front of my car. Rick filled out the report, then left us alone.

Mama and I got back into the car and headed toward town. I was thinking about telling her of the vision I'd had, a vision that had nothing to do with the accident, when another thought came to my mind: I didn't want her to know. The whole thing was so stupid, so confusing. I started rationalizing, justifying, denying.

Mama looked calm, a natural sympathy in her eyes. She patted my arm. "Simone," she asked, "you don't look so hot. Are you okay?"

I nodded. Mama is sweet but she's shrewd, cunning. I imagined that she had been reading my mind so I turned to look out the car window just as we passed Seminole Academy.

It's hard for me to say what was going on inside my head. By the time we got to the hospital, the rain had stopped but the sky had grown darker. We heard the sound of a second ambulance. When it screeched to a stop, two paramedics rushed to help put a lady on a stretcher. The sheet covering her body was bloodstained.

"What happened?" I asked the driver.

His face was lined and weary, but when he recognized us. In a matter-of-fact manner, he replied "Her boyfriend stabbed her," he said.

"How bad?"

"Bad as it can get," he said.

We followed the stretcher into the hospital, then began looking for the young woman I'd hit. She was in a room with a pale green ceiling painted green, faded, and covered with hairline cracks

She sat on the edge of a table. She wore jeans and a lined denim jacket, both smeared with dried blood. On her feet were running shoes and socks. Her eyes darted like she had escaped a trap. She had a broad forehead, arched brows, high cheekbones, a flat nose and generous lips.

The doctor had already taped bandages to her left arm. He was struggling to convince her to stay in the hospital. "We need to check you out," he said.

"I'm getting out of here right now!" she replied, looking me straight in the eyes. A jolt of emotion swept through me, an eruption of heat around my neck and face. "I-it's okay with me," I whispered.

She gripped my arm, and holding onto it, she stood. Her chest heaved and suddenly she was limp and falling. If an orderly, who had walked up behind her, hadn't stepped in, we both would have hit the floor. He lifted her onto a nearby bed.

The doctor, who was a plump-faced man, looked at me. "I'm sorry," he said as the nurse put the IV in her arm. "She'll have to stay and let us check her out now."

"Is she going to be all right?" I asked.

He nodded and frowned. "There aren't any broken bones, but she got hit hard. There could be internal injuries." He hesitated. "In all likelihood, she's in shock," he continued, as if he saw that there was something more that needed to be said. "She'll be all right after a few days. Go home, get some rest. You may not realize it, but you're in shock, too." He opened a nearby cabinet and offered me pills. "Take these," he said. "They'll calm you, help you sleep."

I shook my head.

Mama smiled, her eyes gentle. The doctor looked at me and pointed to his patient. "That's what that young lady over there said."

I reached for the pills. Mama threw her arm around me and led me to the door. She glanced back over her shoulder. "Thanks doctor," she said. "I'll see that she takes them." A few minutes later, Mama and I were in the lobby.

"I've got to call her family," I whispered, "tell somebody that she's here."

"What's her name?" Mama asked.

"I don't know," I answered.

"Admissions will have it," Mama said.

The Admissions' clerk was a small woman with large green eyes and slightly crooked front teeth. "Jane Doe," she said in answer to our inquiry. "That's how we've got her listed in the computer. She wouldn't give her name, had empty pockets, no handbag, nothing!"

I turned to Mama. "Now what?" I asked.

"Back to where you hit her. There's got to be a house nearby. Somebody knows her, knows her people!"

I nodded, thinking of Jane Doe's eyes, and how, like a scent that stirs past memories, our meeting had given me an image from another time, another place. The feeling had been transient, but real. I struggled with the sensation ... *the impression that I too had once been running for my life!*

CHAPTER TWO

The drive down Highway 201 was eerie. The speedometer read 55 mph but I had the feeling that the car was standing still. A mile and a half after I passed the stop sign near Oaktree Crossing, two skid marks on the pavement marked the spot where the young lady had darted out in front of my Honda.

We looked around. There was a mailbox and a dirt road that led beyond a patch of trees. We drove the track that ended at a simple post-and-beam log cabin, a door in the center, a square window on either side of the door. It was surrounded by woods. We parked behind some bushes and walked to the cabin. A padlock hung from a hasp on the door.

We listened, hearing only the usual country sounds of birds and insects. The air was cool but I was sweating; the feeling of dread and tension had returned.

Beyond the house we saw a lake. Well, not really a lake, but a large fishing pond. Anything larger than a puddle is called a lake in that part of the country. We walked through the undergrowth, stepping carefully, lightly, our feet groping the path between the cabin and the water.

There was a flicker in the branches of a nearby tree, a bird, a patch of wildflowers.

"This place is beautiful," I whispered.

Mama looked at the trees, brush and grass. The sound of rushing water floated across the still air. We followed the sound until we reached the bank of a stream. On the opposite side, we could see a house that appeared to have one window. The wind was calm, the sound of birds and rushing water synchronized. We stood listening, watching, drinking in the substance of the atmosphere. The place was hypnotic. There was nobody around, nothing to suggest an intrusion. After a while, we walked to the car in silence, thankful that such a place still existed. "That young lady must have somebody," I said. "There ain't no way she could live out there alone!"

An hour later we were in the warmth of my parents' kitchen. Mama was frying fish. Earlier she had made cole slaw, had taken the baked beans out of the oven and had slipped in a couple of pans of corn bread.

Mama looked thoughtful. "I wonder where that girl was going in such a hurry?" she said.

I scratched my forehead.

"She was running, you know. She ran into your car!"

"Did you see the look in her eyes?" I asked.

Mama was silent, but finally shook her head. "There is something strange about her and I don't like the looks of this," she said, sliding a fresh piece of fish into the hot skillet. "We'll have to talk with her."

I got up from the table, stretched, then moved through the kitchen, automatically touching things. Mama's eyes shifted toward me. "I'm also going to talk to the sheriff," she said. "Tell him about our Jane Doe, let him check out that cabin."

I took a deep breath. "Let me know what he finds," I said, satisfied. "What's for dessert?" I asked, changing the subject.

"Bread pudding," she said, smiling. "I made it last night. All it needs is heating and eating."

Early the next morning I started the drive back to Atlanta. Once I hit Allen and drove onto Highway 125, I passed fields and more patches of old growth forest. The steering wheel quivered like a dowsing rod in my hands; I had the sensation of traveling through a tunnel rather than beautiful countryside. I couldn't shake the sight of the man's face, nor the strange, pungent odor I associated with it. The more I thought about him, the more I felt like I was dragging a weight.

By 3:00 p.m. I was safely home and had called Meredith to tell her that I was coming to her apartment. I met Meredith when Mama and I solved an earlier mystery. When life intrudes, Meredith lets housework slide, forgetting about her unmade bed or loaded dishwasher.

I arrived, greeted her with a kiss, and followed her to the kitchen where she was about to remove a pan of curried goat that had been warming in the oven.

"Girlfriend," I said. "That looks good!"

"Miss Thing," she said, "you don't mind if we eat on paper plates, do you?"

"I didn't mind the last time I ate at your apartment, did I?"

Meredith grinned and changed the subject. "Tell me, how's your people?" she asked, dishing out rice and goat on paper plates that bore the face of Garfield the comic strip cat.

I forced a smile. "Okay."

Meredith looked at me and said quietly. "My child, are you okay?" she asked. "You don't look so good to me."

I nodded. "I'm fine," I said. "I just need a haircut. I'm two weeks overdue."

Meredith grinned and sat down across the table. She leaned forward. "My dear," she said, "your hair is not what's ailing you today!"

I smiled. "Okay, I miss Cliff."

Meredith shrugged. "If that's what you want me to believe, my dear, I will. When will he be back in town?"

"Tuesday."

She scanned my face. "What do you want me to say? It's the pits when your man is away!"

I looked at Meredith and the sight of the man's face, a face that I'd seen someplace before with eyes that bored into me, appeared again. My voice wavered. "I almost killed a woman yesterday," I said, trying to forget the image.

Meredith's mouth fell open. She laid the fork on her plate. "What happened?"

"We were driving, coming from Mama's cousin's house. Mama and I were talking. I took my eyes from the road a second, just a second. When I turned, there she was stepping out in front of my car."

"How bad was she hurt?"

I hesitated. "She's in the hospital."

She frowned slightly, then her expression cleared. "My dear, you need something stronger than coffee," she said. She got up and walked into the kitchen.

"I tried to turn the wheel," I said, loud enough for her to hear me. "Tried to put on the brakes ..."

Meredith returned to the room carrying two glasses of wine. "Sounds like an accident to me. Who is this woman?"

"That's the thing that doesn't sit right. We don't know her name."

"Perhaps she has amnesia?"

I was surprised. "No!"

"What about her pocketbook?" Meredith asked.

I shook my head. "She doesn't want us to know who she is."

"She's got a problem?" Meredith asked.

"Mama and I went to where I hit her. We searched the area. There wasn't anything there."

Meredith's eyes fluttered. "No family?"

"Nothing, nobody. The place was deserted, locked up tight."

Meredith chuckled. "Sounds like Miss Candi's got a mystery on her hands!"

Another tremor of apprehension swept through me. "The woman was scared!"

Meredith's brow knotted. "I guess she would be.

I cut in. "No, I mean scared of something other than the accident."

Meredith sipped from her glass. "What does Miss Candi think?"

"She's going to talk to her."

"Then forget it! Miss Candi will get to the bottom of the whole thing."

I shook my head. "Meredith, I swear Jane Doe was running for her life!"

"You're getting carried away."

I took a bite of goat. "She was scared. I know it!"

Meredith rolled her eyes heavenward. "Girlfriend, don't get started with that protection jazz," she said. "Forget it. She'll be all right!"

I hesitated. "It would be easier if I could tell her relatives, let them watch out for her."

"If she won't tell you her name, you can't find her family, now can you?"

"You know," I said thinking, "her words were a kind of a scream of terror .."

"She was disoriented," Meredith snapped, as she went into the kitchen to get the bottle of wine, "confused."

I raised my voice. "Did I tell you that she passed out when she was trying to leave the hospital?"

"I hope you're not going to become like Miss Candi!" Meredith said, her voice etched with sarcasm. "A seeker of truth and all that stuff. One crusader per family is all that is allowed in this country!"

I said nothing. I didn't want to talk about the vision that connected me to Jane Doe. The sight was a gruesome hint, a reminder of an obscure event, the details of which were hidden in my mind.

Meredith put down her fork and patted my arm again. "Trust me on this one, my child," she said. "When Jane Doe wakes up, she'll be rational, and when she starts thinking about suing you, she'll be glad to tell you her family tree!"

I moved around to the other side of the table and reached for the phone. "Can I call the hospital? I'll use my calling card."

Meredith threw her head back and started laughing. "Child, please," she said. "If that's what it takes, my dear, help yourself!"

After a few sentences, I dropped the receiver on the hook, then turned to face Meredith. "The hospital operator told me that Jane Doe refuses to take any calls," I said.

She raised her eyebrows and studied the glass in her hand. "I'll give you good money, my dear," she said, leaning in her chair, "Miss Jane Doe is thinking insurance. And when she gets it all together, she'll tell you the names of all her kin and she'll pull your heartstrings by telling you that she is their sole support!"

I shook my head.

Meredith snapped impatiently. "The girl will be all right, you'll see."

I shrugged, put the napkin on my plate, then emptied my glass. "You don't understand," I whispered.

CHAPTER THREE

It was Monday morning. I was in my office looking out toward Piedmont Park. My office is one of the few with a really good view of the park. On one wall there is a bookcase and three filing cabinets. Across from that is a couch far enough away from the bookcases that you can go around it to reach books on the lower shelves. Behind my chair is an oak credenza. Its drawers have locks, making it a perfect place for my pocketbook, the tape recorder and confidential files. A built-in computer workstation, a tape player and a few of my cassettes, a few personal, but mostly pertaining to work, are at the left of my desk.

I shivered and took a half step toward the window at the same time that Anna, my boss' secretary, cleared her throat. She had entered quietly. I turned. "I didn't hear you come in."

Anna's voice is modulated with a thick southern accent. She is thin with a stringy neck. She wears her hair in a chopped cut; she has glowing blue eyes. "What time did you come in this morning?" she asked. "When I got here, coffee was made and you had already gone out somewhere."

"I went to get the morning paper," I said, noticing that she had gotten new glasses and wore a different scent. "I like your glasses," I said, deciding not to comment on the perfume; it was too strong. "A big improvement over the Ben Franklin frames perched on the end of your nose."

She touched the side of her face and smiled. "You look tired."

I sighed, then pulled the blinds shut. "I haven't had much sleep. I had an accident over the weekend."

Anna raised her eyebrows. "Child, are you all right?"

I glanced at her and nodded. "I'm okay," I said.

"Anybody hurt?"

"I hit a young woman," I said.

"She ain't dead, is she?"

I took a deep breath. "No, thank goodness, she's not dead."

Anna sat on the edge of the chair. "Car accidents happen every day, nothing to let lay heavy on your mind."

I stared at her. Either I wasn't explaining my feelings or she was insensitive, I thought. "The young lady was scared," I said.

"Child," Anna said, waving her hands, "I wouldn't worry about that." She watched me in silence, then added, "You ain't got time to worry, 'cause, honey, you've got plenty work to do." She shifted and pointed to the envelope that she had placed on my desk, a desk which already contained lab reports, death certificates, and briefs that I had been editing. "Mr. Jacoby left orders for you to work on the Showman case."

I was surprised and not pleased. It wasn't my boss' routine to assign me to a client after he had gone to trial. "The Showman case isn't that big," I said, walking to my desk and sitting down. "Our client will be acquitted."

She coughed, cleared her throat and glanced at her watch. "The boss left orders to give this to you."

I frowned down at my desk, rolled a pencil slowly across its surface. "What does he want?" She shrugged. "He wants you to find him a witness, a Cannon Ferguson."

I straightened up. "Why?"

She waved her hands. "How should I know?" she said, her shoulders hunched and her eyes widening. "He wants you to drop everything and work on finding this man."

I pushed through the paperwork she handed me. "This looks like a detective report."

"It is," she said. "You know the boss, he didn't like not getting what he ordered. He wants Cannon Ferguson, so he's sending you to find him."

"Sounds familiar," I said. I scanned the first page of the report and wondered why Sidney thought I could succeed in finding Cannon Ferguson when his expensive detective failed.

Anna watched me. "Mr. Jacoby likes the way you stick to things," she said. "I guess he uses that high-priced detective because he knows that he's got you as a backup."

I glanced at my watch. It was 9:15. The state traffic department was open and I could call my friend Thelia to track the driver's license. "These documents give me a starting point," I said.

Anna pushed her glasses across her nose. "You're good at piecing things together, finding lost souls," she said, her face bright. "If I were you, I'd get myself a law degree. I bet Mr. Jacoby would make you his partner in a minute."

I shook my head. "No thanks," I said.

The truth is that I'd considered law school many times but decided against it. It's one thing to fill out forms, connect dates, or track down people on paper for Sidney. It's another to stand in front of a jury and try to convince them that a person is innocent and shouldn't be sent to the electric chair. And another truth is, I've always thought corporate law would as boring."

"How long will Sidney be out of town?" I asked.

"One little week," she said, pausing awkwardly halfway out the door. Her forehead wrinkled. "It ain't worth the price of a plane ticket, but the trip ain't for pleasure; it's part of what's happening with the Showman case." She paused. "By the way, your mechanic called."

I frowned, waited until she had gone before I picked up the phone, then dialed my mechanic's shop. It took me forty-five minutes to negotiate an estimate for my Honda's repair. After that, I read the detective's report.

Sidney had used his one-man outfit, Leonard Leslie to look for Cannon Ferguson. We both knew that Leonard did a lot of padding and got little results. In this case, he charged hundreds of dollars for time spent searching for the birth certificate of Cannon Ferguson. He didn't find one. I sighed. It's common to have a mother's name, birth date and a place of birth, and still not find a certificate. Usually, with a little effort, I'd find an affidavit filed when the person tried to get a birth certificate and found that it didn't exist because of an incompetent midwife.

Leonard had been given Cannon Ferguson's last known address. There were two pages of unflattering descriptions of the frame house, but no Cannon Ferguson. Leonard said he had canvassed schools around Atlanta and had come up with one Cannon Ferguson, but he had died before he finished high school. After a while, I shuffled the typed sheets together and put them back into the envelope. I made a few phone calls. Around 3:00 p.m. the phone rang. I picked it up thinking that it was some of my contacts returning my call. "Simone?" the voice said, almost out of breath.

"Mama, where are you? What's happened?" I asked.

Mama spoke rapidly. "I'm at my office," she said. "Somebody just came in the building and said that a man walked into Otis General a few minutes ago, put a gun to Jane Doe's head and pulled the trigger!"

For a few seconds I remembered thinking that my worst fears had been realized. "Is she dead?"

There was a lot of background noise, I could barely hear Mama's words. "I don't know!" she said. Someone interrupted her; she put her hand over the receiver.

"Simone," Mama's voice returned.

"What's going on?"

"I'm not sure. Another employee just came into the office and said that the woman isn't dead. There's so much commotion around here, so much confusion!"

"Where were the hospital guards?"

Mama's voice was muffled. "I'll call you back as soon as I get the truth about what happened."

"Find out if she's dead!"

"Okay, okay," Mama said, anxious to get me off the phone.

I sat for an hour in a trance, staring. There was something wrong with the picture in my head. I didn't see the girl's face but the man's face, the same man that I'd seen when I looked into her eyes. He was putting a gun against Jane Doe's head, his hand pulling the trigger. I sat trying to adjust the picture in my mind when the phone rang again.

"Simone," Mama said, her voice less urgent.

"Yes."

"I'm at the hospital and Sheriff Abe has arrived. Everything has calmed down."

"What happened?"

She took a deep breath and let it out slowly. "It's

not as bad as it was reported."

I pressed the receiver close to my ear. "She's not dead?"

"No, she's not dead. The nurse said that a man showed up looking for her."

My office felt airless, too warm. My heart was pounding as if it was going to leap right out of my chest.

"When he found her, he pulled a gun and threatened the nurse and doctor who were in the room with her. He took Jane Doe from the hospital but he didn't shoot anybody. After they were in the car, he drove off toward Yemassee!"

"Did anybody see the car?" I asked.

"The nurse. It was blue, four-door, but things happened so fast that nobody got the number on the license plate."

"Anybody describe him?"

"A lady told me that he was a tall black man, about thirty, broad shoulders, black hair, cut short."

This wasn't the man appearing in my visions. "I suppose he'll kill her now that he's got her," I said.

Mama took a deep breath and let it out. "I don't think he wants to kill her."

"Why?"

"He could have killed her right there in the hospital."

I interrupted. "I don't know."

Mama was silent. "I think he wants her for another reason."

My heart pounded; I felt confused.

"Relax," Mama said. "Let me give this some thought and I'll get back to you."

I put the phone on its receiver, then swallowed three aspirins with a mouthful of cold coffee when the strange smell I associated with the vision of the man came to me again. This time when I saw the man's face, I got the impression that he had some kind of sickness. One thing was for sure, he was not the one who had snatched the young lady from the hospital, not the one that tied me and Jane Doe together. Then in a voice I could barely recognize, I heard myself whisper, *"Please don't kill me!"*

CHAPTER FOUR

It had been a hectic week. I'd tracked a man who was an expert at hiding. Cannon Ferguson had changed his name and moved from Atlanta to Alabama, from there to Tennessee, and then to Florida, where he'd lived three years. When he returned to Atlanta, he once again changed his name, this time to Clay Ferguson. Fortunately, he left a paper trail that led to his address in Jonesboro, a town a few miles outside of metro Atlanta. I called Sidney's detective and dropped the ball in his lap again.

I hadn't been so busy that I failed to snatch a couple of phone calls a day to check on Jane Doe. Mama had no news. We suspected that nobody was really looking for the girl. If I just had a name to go on, I was sure I could find her.

Normally, I love driving. It's a good time for thinking. Not this morning. It was 6:05 a.m. and I was driving east on Interstate 20 again. As daylight approached, I let my mind be absorbed by the moving silhouettes of the countryside until there was a cloudless sky. Today I struggled with my memory. A part of me ached to forget the pungent odor I couldn't quite identify and the man's bony and evil face. The other insisted on remembering, demanding confrontation. I hadn't seen the vision for a few days but I knew it was there, strengthening, and waiting for the right time to come back.

I passed through Augusta and crossed the South Carolina state line, where I picked up Highway 125 to the 278 which angled toward the sea, through Allendale, Fairfax and on into Otis. Today the trip took longer than usual and it was 10:00 when I finally reached Otis and passed the courthouse with its huge fountain. A few minutes later, I was in my parents' front yard.

Mama was in the kitchen. She was wearing a beautifully embroidered apron and met me with the coffee pot in her hand. The wonderful smell of toast, eggs, bacon and grits and chocolate almond coffee filled the room. When Mama leaned across the table I saw a stirring of suspicion in her dark, curious eyes. She smiled, set a mug of coffee in front of me and whispered, "You all right? You don't look so hot."

I opened my mouth to answer but the back door opened and my father walked inside. I stood up for my hug. He put his arms around me and squeezed. "How's my girl?" he asked.

"I'm okay."

His brows went up. "Candi tells me that you ran into a girl last week."

I nodded.

"I guess you're upset about that crazy man going into the hospital in broad daylight and snatching her away."

I pulled away and sat in my chair. "It is strange, don't you think?"

He waited for a second, then shook his head. "We live in a strange world." He changed the subject. "How's your Honda?" he asked.

"It took the whole thing pretty well. I negotiated with my mechanic and I think I did a fair job of it."

Daddy looked guarded. "He probably charged you an arm and a leg," he said.

"It wasn't cheap for a little bent fender but I got it fixed."

He took a deep breath, then let it out. "I'd better check it out before you leave, make sure it's all right."

I tried to smile. My father's face and voice were serious even though I knew that his inspection was more for his ego than for my car.

"You don't look so hot," he said as an afterthought. "That boy Cliff treating you right?"

I nodded.

"How did he let you leave him in Atlanta for the weekend?" he asked.

"Cliff's not in Atlanta."

"He's gone again?" Mama asked.

I nodded. "You know," I said, changing the subject, "it's hard to believe that someone would walk into a hospital and take that girl."

Daddy interrupted, his head tilted to one side. "I told Candi I'll give you two to one they're in it together," he said.

My eyebrows rose. "In what together?"

Daddy shrugged, his face uncertain. "In whatever they're running from!"

My shoulders sagged.

Daddy rubbed his chin. "My hunch is that they're running from the law, or some drug ring."

Mama looked across the table and leaned forward. "I wouldn't be surprised if you're right," she said, looking into my eyes. "I've given it a lot of thought and I've come to the conclusion that there is more to the girl than meets the eye."

I sipped my coffee. "I could never figure out how you come up with such conclusions as that. You didn't even talk to that girl," I snapped.

"Okay," Mama said, a bit of defiance in her tone, "what do you think about Jane Doe?"

"I think she's on the run from somebody, and it's not the law!" I said.

"She told you that?" Mama asked.

I remembered Jane Doe's face. "She told me something," I said.

"What exactly?" Mama said.

"It was when you went to the car to get the umbrella."

"What?"

"She said, 'This ain't nothing like what's going to happen to me if I don't get away from this place!,'" I said, "and the way she said it sounded like she was on the run from a person, not the law!"

Daddy shook his head. "I still don't buy it," he said. "My money is on the two of them being in something illegal together."

"You didn't see the look in her eyes, didn't hear

the fear in her voice."

Mama look skeptical. "I saw her," she said. "There wasn't anything about her looks that gave me the impression that she was scared. Are you sure you're reading her right?"

I was annoyed. "We won't know until we find her, will we?" I snapped.

Mama smiled. "I talked Abe into giving us permission to look for her in his mug books."

Daddy look irritated. "Why don't you forget the whole thing?" he asked.

"It's the right thing to do," Mama said. "If that good-for-nothing who took her away from the hospital is out to hurt her, it's right that we help her!"

Daddy shook his head like he knew it was useless to try to change Mama's mind. He walked to the door and reached for the door handle. "You drive your car, Candi. I want to check the Honda."

Mama nodded and smiled, her teeth white against her golden skin. I was tempted to tell her how glad I was that she was going to stick with me on this one, but then I'd have to give my reason and I wasn't ready for that.

A few hours later, Mama and I were in Sheriff Abe's small office combing through books of mug shots. Nobody looked familiar. I had to make myself look at the pictures because something in the back of my mind nagged that I'd seen Jane Doe's face before, and it wasn't in the post office on a Wanted Poster.

We had been in the sheriff's office for forty-five

minutes. "This thing doesn't make much sense," I said.

Mama leaned forward, a curious look in her eyes. "You believe that Jane Doe is in trouble ... big trouble?"

I nodded.

"You're determined to find her?"

I swallowed. "Yeah!"

"If I didn't know you better, I'd think you were the one scared," she said.

I took a deep breath. "What would I be scared of?"

Mama patted my arm. "I know you, something is wrong."

I cut in. "I'm worried about the girl, that's all!" I snapped.

Mama smiled. "Why are you so defensive?"

"I'm not defensive. That girl was scared that the man will kill her."

Mama looked startled. She stared at me for a moment. "The girl told you that somebody was trying to kill her?"

I shook my head but said nothing. The realization that the girl hadn't said anything about somebody trying to kill her felt eerie. I began looking in the book again. One page held two photographs of women, their eyes cut out. "This is a waste of time." I said.

Mama cut in. "Can you think of anything better to do?"

I started looking in the book again. A pair of eyes glared at me; I returned its stare when a pressure began to build, the feeling that you get between the time that a firecracker has been lit and the time it explodes. Words collided in my head:Will ... Jane Doe!

Mama looked puzzled. "You recognize somebody?" she asked.

I swallowed, her words bringing together faces which my mind wanted separated.

"Simone," she asked. "What's the matter?"

I hesitated, not sure how she was going to take what I had realized. I took a deep breath and decided to spit the words out as fast as I could. "We won't find the girl's picture in these books!" I said.

Mama leaned across the desk, her face and body slack, her voice soft. "You know who she is, don't you?"

Again, things were quiet. Mama's dark eyes held me in their gaze. I closed the book. "Let's forget the whole thing," I said.

Mama's face took on a determined look, a tenacity that I'd seen before.

I took a deep breath. "She's a friend of Will's," I said.

Mama laughed. "My son Will?"

I nodded. "I remember seeing her in Will's photo album," I said.

Mama gazed once more at the books.

I continued. "He sent home a box of his things before he left to go overseas."

"That had to be over six years ago," Mama said. "He's been married five years."

"It was before he got married," I said. "There was a camera, pictures and ..." My voice trailed.

Mama sat looking at me. "That was a long time ago, Simone," she said, her voice lowered. "You sure you saw that girl's picture in Will's photo album? The same girl?"

I closed my eyes. "I think so ... yes," I whispered. "I'm sure. She's in a picture with Will and another soldier."

Mama straightened up. "Then we're looking in the wrong place," she said, her tone curt. "Let's go home and find Will's old photo album!"

CHAPTER FIVE

Mama's attic is a large room with a sleeping loft over the kitchen. Books are jammed and stacked into shelves that line one wall. Bundles of magazines are on both sides of a window. A table in the corner is covered with mounds of records. An old stereo and suitcases lean against another wall.

"Where do we start?" I asked.

Mama walked over to the books and began straightening things on the shelf. "Do you remember which album belongs to Will?" she asked. I went through a mass of albums. There were strips of paper protruding up from the pages, like the tabs on file folders. I was surprised to see how many pictures had been marked with both names and dates. On the floor next to the table lay a thick scrapbook, its cover had embossed letters that read, Will Covington. I picked it up and rested it on my lap. The first part were pictures of Will when he was in basic training. The second contained the picture I remembered.The girl in the picture was the same, her hair was cut short, she wore glasses, the weightless frames giving her a scholarly look. She was thinner, dressed in jeans, a white blouse, a red leather belt. Her almost-white skin, her broad forehead, arched brows, high cheekbones, flat nose and generous lips were unmistakable. My heart was in my throat. "This is it," I whispered. "This is the picture!"

"Are you sure?" Mama asked.

I was sure. The picture held the same magnetism that pulled me toward the strange pun gent smell and the ailing man. "If this photo is five years old, it would make her almost twenty-five now."

"Let's just hope that Will remembers her name," she said.

The ring of the doorbell startled us.

I grabbed the picture.

"What time is it?" Mama asked.

"Three-thirty."

"Wonder who that can be?"

I followed Mama downstairs and opened the front door.

Her cousin Hester was standing in the doorway. "Fingers has been locked up," she said, her voice desperate.

"Come in the kitchen," Mama said. "I'll get some coffee."

Mama's kitchen had been recently remodeled, the new appliances were black, counters and cabinets white, the wallpaper an Oriental pattern of pastel flowers against delicate blue.

"I knew something like this would happen," I said. "It was just a matter of time."

Hester cut in. She was rubbing her hands up the

sides of her arms. "Fingers ain't never took nothing from a store before," she said.

"Calm yourself, Hester," Mama said, as she poured Hester a cup of flavored coffee, then pulled a chair close to her and sat down.

Hester lowered her head. "I don't know what to do," she said. "Fingers is just a boy and I know he's scared."

"Is he in Abe's jail?" Mama asked.

Hester looked up and shook her head. "He's in Hillsdale," she said, blinking back tears.

Mama took a deep breath and drew her eyebrows together. I could see that Hester's expression had pricked her heart. When Mama spoke her voice was empathic, soft. "It would have been easier if Abe had him."

Hester's eyes pleaded.

"You'll need a lawyer," I said.

"I ain't got no money for a lawyer. I shouldn't need a lawyer for a boy."

Mama interrupted. "The family will have to come up with money for Fingers' lawyer," she said. "We're as much to blame as you are. We should've been honest with you before now, should've made you get help for the boy!"

"Me and my boy are happy! Fingers doesn't mean any harm, you know that, Candi!"

"That's not the point," I said.

Hester looked past me, her lips parted and her eyes wide.

"Did Fingers take anything out of the store before the manager caught him?" Mama asked.

Hester rolled her eyes. "No," she said quickly.

"That's why I don't know why they're keeping him. Fingers never got anything out of that store!"

"He would have if he hadn't gotten caught," I said.

Hester jumped up and started pacing, rubbing the palms of her hands together. "Fingers doesn't mean no harm. Candi, you tell them, he's always ready to give back whatever he picks up, ain't he?"

Mama nodded. "That may work with the family, Hester, but Fingers has graduated to taking things from other people, and they're not so understanding."

Hester sat down and started crying, the veins popping in her forehead. "I don't know what to do! Candi, you know there's nobody but me and Fingers. He's so young."

"He's young, but give him a few more years and he'll be smart enough to use his little problem profitably."

Hester looked up. "Shut up!" she shouted.

I knew this was no time to lecture, but I also knew that someone needed to speak to her honestly. "Hester, your son's mind is sick and when the mind is sick, it shows in different ways. It's worse than something being physically wrong with him because you can't take X-rays, can't operate, can't ...

Hester rubbed her hands together. "Fingers ain't sick! Ain't nothing wrong with his brains!"

"If you don't want this to happen again," I said, "you're going to have to admit that he has a problem and help him!"

Hester hid her face in her hands, then suddenly she was standing. She was so thin, couldn't have weighed more than a hundred pounds. Wrinkles zigzagged from her eyes. She reminded me of a frightened bird. She reached for a paper towel and blew her nose, then she took another and blotted her face. She stared, then walked toward the window where she stood, her arms crossed beneath her breasts. "When Fingers gets out of this mess, I'll watch him more carefully," she said. "I promise, I won't let this happen to my boy again."

"Our problem now is to get Fingers out of jail. After that, we'll talk about getting help for him. Simone, you think Sidney can get him bail?"

I blew out a long, loud breath. "It's almost four-thirty on a Saturday afternoon; I have no idea where to find Sidney or whether he can do anything."

Mama stood up and walked to the telephone. "Then I'll call Abe," she said. "He knows the sheriff in Crawford County."

Four hours later, we were on Highway 363 heading to Hillsdale. Mama drove, I sat on the passenger's side. Hester climbed into the back seat.

The evening was cold with heavy broken clouds darting across the sky. he scenery slipped by the window, the new moon highlighting the skirting farms and fields.

Right after we pulled on Highway 363, Hester spoke. "I heard about your car wreck," she said, a chuckle of derision in her voice now that Sheriff

Abe had arranged for Fingers to be released. I thought how easy it was for her to forget her son's actions; how easy it was to believe that his release was the only problem they both faced.

I turned from the window. "Yeah," I said, thinking about the picture I had gotten from Will's album.

Hester cocked her head. "The nurses and doctors say that the woman wanted to leave the hospital," she said. I shifted in my seat.

"I guess a lot of people think that way," I said. She nodded.

"The same thing happened six years ago," she said. "The exact same thing!"

We were approaching the fork that led off to Madison. I turned to look at Hester, who sat grinning. Mama straightened up and pulled herself toward the steering wheel. She tapped the brakes. "What do you mean? " she asked.

Hester took a deep breath, then let it out slowly. "Somebody, I think it was Hank James. I don't know. he hit a woman on the road from Madison. He called the ambulance and they took her to the hospital. She was hurt pretty bad so they didn't get to taking her name or who she belonged to when they admitted her. The next morning, she had disappeared without a trace. Nobody remembered seeing her the entire night." Her voice was contemplative. "If she was in as bad a shape as they say she was, she couldn't walk out of that hospital by herself. Somebody got her, too!"

"Somebody walked into the hospital in the middle of the night and took the girl?" I asked.

Hester's eyes darted between us. "I reckon so," she said, her tone light. "At least that's what people said. What do you think, Candi?"

Mama lifted her chin. "I don't know, Hester," she said.

"If my mind serves me right, you and James had moved home when it happened."

Mama turned her head toward her side mirror. "I don't remember hearing about it."

"That's right," Hester said. "Now I remember. You and James were getting your house built. Still, you should have heard about it."

Mama shook her head. "I don't remember hearing anything."

My heart pounded. "What did the sheriff do?"

"Abe went through the area trying to find out if anybody knew the young woman, but nobody claimed any knowledge of her."

"Maybe she was from out of town," I said.

Hester smiled. "I don't think so."

"Abe dropped the search without finding her?" I asked.

"I reckon most folks forgot about the girl and, after a while, Abe did too."

I turned to Mama. "I'm surprised that he didn't mention the similarity of that situation to us," I said.

We crossed the line in Crawford County. Mama cleared her throat; neither of us spoke again. I sat with my head toward the window. The clouds whipped overhead like black ships, the moon sliding behind one, then peeking out, then going down again.

When we reached Hillsdale, Mama eased up on the accelerator, pushed her hands against the steering wheel and pulled onto Main Street. She drove to the corner and made a turn to head into the center of the town. She parked some fifty yards from the jail.

I had the feeling that Mama's intuition was working, but for a moment, when we stepped outside of the car and smelled the smoke from a dry-wood fire, I forgot about it.

CHAPTER SIX

The next morning, Mama called and invited Will and his family home for a weekend. Several hours later, the details had been worked out. Will would be home in two weeks. It would be a time of festivity. Mama would cook and I'd invite Ernest, Yasmine, Meredith and Cliff.

My parents' dining room has a floral theme with a generous mix of ceramics and doilies. On the hardwood floor lay an enormous Persian rug that Mama bought when Daddy was stationed in North Africa. The large mahogany dining table with its ten chairs sits in the middle of the rug and is donned with a lace tablecloth hand-made in the West Indies. Today it was set with hand-carved crystal bowls, three beautiful crystal meat platters, and silver salt-and-pepper shakers along with Mama's china, crystal and silver service. The usual bouquet of dried flowers was the centerpiece.

A silver coffee pot with ivory handles sat on the glass table near Mama's chair. My father was at the head of the table. My brother, his wife and their five-year-old twins were on his right;

Yasmine, Ernest, Meredith, Cliff and I sat at his left. Mama was at the other end, close to the pantry. She looked satisfied with the results of the hours it had taken her to cook. A pang of jealousy swept through me. I felt it every time we were in the company of my brothers because my mother looks happiest when she's done her thing for them, when she's cooked what they want to eat.

The room was warm with the aroma of baked chicken, dressing, baked ham, fried chicken, collard greens, okra, corn and tomatoes, candied sweet potatoes, rice, potato salad, corn bread and homemade yeast rolls. For desert, Will had requested carrot, red velvet and coconut cakes.

The conversation centered around the military with Will expounding on exploits that were familiar to him and my father. I wanted to change the subject, so I blurted, "Fingers was arrested!"

My sister-in-law Ruth looked startled. "Who is Fingers?" she asked, her voice so soft I could hardly hear it.

Will was embarrassed. "Fingers is Hester's boy. She's Mama's second cousin," he explained. "So, I guess you can say he's a very distant third cousin." Will took a deep breath, then pointed his fork in my direction. "It's your story," he said, "you tell her."

I smiled, thinking how uncomfortable Will was whenever somebody talked about those whom he considered to be tarnished relatives.

Cliff asked, "Why do you all call him Fingers?"

"He's a kleptomaniac," I said.

Every one's eyebrows rose but Will's . "He's not

such a bad kid," he said. "He's always given up his wares whenever he's been caught, right Mama?"

Mama smiled. "Yes," she said. "That may work for the family, but not for a store owner."

"I can't believe that Hester let him swipe something from a store."

"She can't stop him." I said.

Daddy sighed. "Candi said it was a piece of ten-cent candy, something Hester could have paid for."

"Hester better do something," I said, trying to remember what Fingers' father looked like.

Mama sighed. "Simone," she said staring at me, "don't let Hester's problem spoil our meal."

Will's eyes locked with Mama's. He winked, satisfied that she had stifled me. I was thinking about Hester and my older brothers when Cliff said, "Well, so much for the family gossip."

Everybody, except my niece who was staring up at the ceiling, was eating.Will, Jr. spoke excitedly. "Granddaddy," he said, his mouth full of sweet potatoes, "I won a trophy!"

Daddy paused. He was buttering a piece of a roll. "You did?," he asked.

"Don't talk with your mouth full," Ruth said quietly.

The child chewed his food, then swallowed. "Karate," he said when he could speak. "I won first place in my tournament."

"I don't like him taking that," Ruth said in a tone reminiscent of my mother's whenever she disagreed with a course my father had set for his own sons.

Will frowned. "I told you," he said, separating a piece of chicken from its skin, "it'll make a man out of him."

Daddy smiled, and munched on his roll, all the while avoiding Mama's eyes. "I'm proud of you," he said to Will, Jr. "I'll have to give you something special."

"I won a prize, too," my niece stuttered.

Ruth smiled. "She's taking ballet," she said. "She's doing good in her class."

"My teacher said that I'm doing great," the child said.

Ruth smiled but Will seemed preoccupied with getting as much chicken in his mouth as he could.

"After dinner," I said to my niece, "I have something special for you, too."

She shook her head. "See, Will," she said beaming, "they like me, too!"

"We love both of you," Mama said. "And we're very proud of both of you!"

Will, Jr.'s eyes glittered. "Granddaddy likes me 'cause I'm going into the army just like he did."

Will glanced at his son, but didn't say anything.

I cleared my throat. "Sari," I said to my niece, "you've got a tradition to keep, too." I smiled. "You can be the family's third generation of female detectives."

"I can!" she said, then stuck her tongue out at her brother.

My sister-in-law laughed. "You and your mother are still sneaking around in the woods looking for corpses?" she asked.

"We haven't been out in the woods lately," I said. "This time we're looking for somebody who is alive!"

Mama's head shook every so slightly and she hit my calf with her foot while we talked. I got her message loud and clear; she didn't want me to mention the girl in Will's picture just yet.

For the first time Ernest put his fork down. He leaned back in his chair. "You mean you're not trying to solve a murder?" he asked.

"No," Mama said, "we're not trying to solve a murder."

"Then you're not having fun," he said, pointing toward the dessert tray.

"Maybe," I said, "we'll save somebody from being murdered!"

"That's cool, too," Ernest said.

Mama, who had stood up and walked over to the dessert table, cut Ernest a slice and served him. "Anybody else?" she asked. "Tell me before I sit down."

The orders came fast. It was several minutes before everyone had cake in front of them. Donna took up the dialogue again. "Simone, tell Will and Ruth about your accident."

I reached for my fork. "I had an accident a little over a month ago."

Daddy stood up, offering wine.

Will looked concerned. "You all right?" he asked.

"I'm fine," I said. "I hit a young lady."

"She's hurt bad?" he asked, shifting in his chair, looking at me, eyes wide, serious.

"She had to be hospitalized," I said. I was thinking about the face of the young woman, a face which been so imprinted on my mind that I remembered seeing her and Will together in a six-year-old photograph.

Will's eyebrows arched. I glanced at my coffee, realizing that he was waiting for me to say more. "I don't think she's hurt," I said.

Will looked at my father, who nodded.

"The strange thing is that a man came and snatched her out of the hospital. Nobody knows who she is or who her people are."

Will rubbed his stomach. "Sounds like something that happened around these parts one time before," he said, his jaws grinding on a piece of cake.

Mama looked intrigued. When she spoke, her voice was tight, noticeably so by those of us who know her well. "You remember that incident?" she asked.

Will took another bite, chewed and swallowed. "It was when you and Daddy were having this house built, don't you remember?"

Mama shook her head. There was a silence. Will considered. You and Daddy were here for two weeks, I came for one weekend."

Daddy sipped from his glass. "We were having such a time with the contractor," he reflected. "I guess everything else that was going on went over our heads, right, Candi?"

Mama asked, "What do you remember?"

Will pushed his fork into the red devil cake. "Not much," he said. "There was some talk about a girl who got hit by a car, they put her in the hospital and sometime during the night she disappeared." He waved his fork.

"That's it?"

"Did you know the girl?" I asked.

He shook his head, chewed and swallowed. "The reason I mentioned it is because it sounds like what happened to your girl," he said.

Several hours later the fireplace in the family room had dispersed enough heat to provide moderate warmth throughout the room. Cliff, Ernest and Donna had gone to the motel. Meredith was sound asleep in my bed. My niece and nephew had been put to bed. Ruth, whose habit it is to snatch quiet time to read, dismissed herself, leaving my parents, Will and me sitting in front of the fire sipping the last of the wine.

"It's good to be home," Will said.

I smiled, thinking how seldom he visited. "There's a lot to be said for the comfort and familiarity of this house," I said.

Will looked embarrassed and, as is typical, Mama helped him by changing the subject. "When was the last time you spoke to your brother?" she asked.

Will looked more self-conscious. "I'm sorry to say that I don't remember, it's been a long time."

Mama looked a bit tense. "Call him when you get to your base," she said.

Will tipped his glass and smiled. "That's a promise," he said.

"Will ," I said, ready to address the picture of the girl. "About six years ago you sent home a box of your things."

"So?"

"There was a picture of you, a guy and a girl."

"Simone," he said, "I can't remember what I had for breakfast yesterday, how do you ..."

Mama interrupted. "Will," she said, "it's important that you remember."

Will looked surprised. Mama's tone was serious, almost as deliberate as when she tried to discourage him from going into the Army. He sat up straight. "Okay," he said, "I sent a box, what about it?"

"I want you to look at the picture and tell me the name of the girl," I said.

"Why?"

"Because she's the girl I hit," I said.

His eyebrows rose and I stood up, reached into my purse and pulled out the picture. Mama seemed to be holding her breath. Will leaned forward, shrugged, then grinned. "I don't remember her name," he said.

"Do you know whether or not she was from around here?" I asked.

"The thing I know is that my buddy Hank James said he was going to marry the girl." He lifted his glass. Mama's shoulders slumped. Will closed his eyes and sipped again from his glass. He smiled, like he felt a rush; one hand lifted like he remembered something important. "Come to think of it, I ran into Hank the same weekend that I mentioned at the dinner table," he said.

My heart pounded.

Mama asked, "When this house was being

built?"

"Yeah," he said. "I saw him come out of Piggley Wiggley in Panola but I didn't talk to him."

"Was the girl with him?" I asked.

He hesitated, thinking. "No," he said, "he was by himself."

CHAPTER SEVEN

A week had passed. My brother had gone back to Orlando. Cliff was in California again, Ernest and Yasmine had driven to Florida to attend a funeral. Meredith had flown to the Bahamas to visit her family. I was alone in Atlanta.

I did my twenty-minute workout, then ate my microwave lasagna. Later I studied my face in the water-spotted mirror above the sink in my bathroom, then took a shower hoping that hot water would ease my feelings. When I left the bathroom and dressed in a long cotton flannel nightgown, I still felt the sensation, saw the man's face again. It was powerful!

I sat on the sofa watching TV and folding clothes that had been washed earlier. The lead story was about an airliner that had crashed, killing all 128 passengers. I flipped to another channel, then pushed the off button.

I walked to the window where, for the next few minutes, I stood staring out. Being alone wasn't what I needed!

I frowned. My thoughts were on the girl and the vision that she had brought into my life. Before the accident, I doubted that anything or anybody could have been so compelling. I was just not the type to feel psychic. I shut my eyes. Despair came in a surge, a wave. I opened my eyes and straightened my body.

I turned, walked into my bedroom and switched on the lights. After I drew the blinds, I flopped down on my four-poster bed and closed the eyes on my face and opened the one in my mind. The odor, the man's face and Chloe's words rushed me again. I cleared my throat and wondered what made me think that if I found the girl, I'd find my man.

The phone rang.

"It's snowing," I said, after hearing my mother's voice. "Streets are closed."

"I heard," she said. "That's why I'm calling. You all right?"

"Everybody is out of town. I'm nursing a serious attitude!"

"Well," Mama suggested, "when the weather breaks, you come home and we'll visit Madison. I've tracked down Will's friend Hank. A woman t I work with told me that he married a girl from Madison. I figure if we go down the strip showing the picture, somebody might remember her."

"It's supposed to warm up later tonight," I said. "If it does, I'll be home tomorrow."

I had trouble falling asleep that night. I lay in the bed and tried to trick my body into fatigue, consciously relaxing muscles, forcing my breathing to slow and deepen, but every time I shut my eyes, the same images floated before me.

Saturday's temperatures rose to fifty and everything began to melt in a dripping, sliding, oozing rush. By mid-day, white clouds floated across the sky pushed gently northward by the touch of a wind. It was after three when I got in my car and drove toward I-20, east. I wouldn't be in Otis until seven, but it was better than sitting alone in my apartment and nursing a dark mood.

The next afternoon, my mother and I visited the small area of Madison located five miles on the other side of Chambers. The row of shanties that lined the railroad track once housed people who worked in the sawmill.

We talked to a few folks before we were directed to a red board house at the end of the track. After explaining our mission, we were invited into a large room by Martha Benton, a woman who had fair skin and determined gray hair that straggled about her face. She looked numb and lifeless. Her shoulders were bent, her gray head sunk between them. She shuffled with deliberation to a chair that appeared to be both comfortable and hers. She folded her arms, forcing her bosoms upward, so that they looked like a pair of balloons. "Where you folks from?" she asked.

The room we sat in looked like it had been furnished in the twenties. It contained two big chairs, a brown sofa, worn rugs, a large chest, a large wood heater and a stack of wood piled high on a back wall.

Mama sat on a chair, I sat on the couch, an air of expectancy circled the room. "I live in Otis," Mama said.

Martha Benton examined us with dark eyes. "I don't like strangers about me," she said.

"If I call some of my people's names, you'll know them," Mama said.

Martha Benton stared at Mama, then nodded. "Like who?" she asked.

"My grandmother was Sandra Jones and ..."

Martha Benton cut in. "You look like some people who used to live on the other side of Kent," she said.

"Some of my people," Mama said.

Martha stared.

"Look at this picture," I said, anxious to get to the purpose of our visit.

Martha unfolded her arms and took the picture, tilting it at a crazy angle. "Looks like my girl Chloe," she said, her voice southern. "'Course my eyes ain't what they used to be."

I smiled. "We're trying to find her," I said.

Martha leaned forward. To my surprise, her eyes brimmed with tears. "He took Chloe away from me when she was a baby, but I'm the woman that birthed her in this world and she had to know it." She took a deep breath as if trying to control tears. She straightened her face with an effort, fishing in her pocket for a rag she used as a handkerchief.

Mama smiled. "How long has it been since she's known that you're her mother?" she asked.

Martha's eyes widened. "I don't know, four, maybe five years, why?"

Mama's smile was warm. "No reason," she whispered.

The old woman looked at me with the wide-eyed innocence of a school child.

"Mrs. Benton," Mama said, "the reason we're looking for your daughter is because my daughter," she pointed at me, "accidentally hit her about six weeks ago. We put her in the hospital, but a few days later a man came and took her out before we had a chance to talk to her. We want to know if she is okay, if there is anything else we can do to help her."

A hint of irritation flashed across Martha's face. She was wearing a red housecoat and I could see the muscles tighten along her jaw. "My girl ain't been hit with a car 'cause she ain't been home for a good while now!"

"Give me her phone number," I pressed. "I'd like to talk with her."

The woman blew her nose. "I talked to Chloe less than an hour ago. If she of had been hit by a car, she'd would've said something about it!"

"Maybe if we ..."

Martha Benton cut in, her jaw tight. "I ain't giving you Chloe's phone number!" she said. "I don't know who you are or what you're looking for, but you can't prove that my Chloe is mixed up in anything!"

"We're not accusing your daughter ."

"Then don't be asking questions about her!" she said.

"We just ..."

Martha cut in again. "You better get out of here!" she snapped.

Mama hesitated, then stood up. Martha

Benton's hostility was unnerving. Still, something made me pull out one of my business cards, write my home phone number on it and hand it to her. "When you talk to your daughter again, ask her to call me, collect."

Martha Benton didn't say any more. I put the card on a nearby table and glanced toward Mama, who nodded, then followed me to the door.

"The way she acted, you'd think that Chloe was involved in something illegal," I said when we were sitting in the car.

"I'm sure of one thing," Mama said. "She doesn't want us to talk to her daughter."

I swallowed, turned the key in the ignition and headed toward Otis.

The next morning I was back in Atlanta. I reached the office at eight o'clock, settled behind my desk, seeing Chloe's face and sharing her fear. I was sick. My best efforts had failed, something that I found as hard to deal with as Cliff's constant absence. Everything I wanted evaded me, I thought. All I've got is a shattered memory, a sickening fear, a faceless man, an evasive woman and the pleading of Chloe!

I put the key in my computer, then reached for the phone. I dialed the number for the Bureau of Vital Statistics in Columbia, South Carolina. A few minutes later I was talking to a friend who felt no qualms in faxing me copies of birth certificates for a small honorarium.

"Who are you looking for now?" she asked when she heard my voice.

"Chloe Benton," I said. "She's between twenty-five or thirty, may have been born in Otis County."

She interrupted. "Wait a minute," she said, "give me time to write this down."

"I need it as soon as possible," I said.

"Your boss on to something hot?"

"No," I admitted. "This is something I'm working on privately."

"You're getting good at this," she said. "Maybe you'll open up your own practice."

"I don't think so," I said. "Lately, I'm not getting anything I want!"

"What else can you tell me about Chloe Benton," she said.

"Check the spelling," I said. "To be honest, I'm pulling for straws, but sooner or later I've got to find something!"

"How much of a donation can I expect if I find her?" she asked.

"Fifty dollars for a look, one hundred for a find."

"You've got it," she said.

I put the receiver down, absorbed in my own thoughts.

An hour later, my phone rang. When the party on the other end cleared her throat, I knew I had hit pay dirt. "You found her?" I asked.

"Chloe Benton was born in Otis County on June 26, 19--." she said.

"Her mother's name?" I asked.

"Martha Benton."

"Good work," I said. "Fax me a copy. Your check is in today's mail."

"Wait a minute," she said. "That's not all you're getting for your money."

I hesitated. "There's more?"

"Chloe Benton has been dead for five years. She died in Otis County on July 7, 19--!"

CHAPTER EIGHT

My eyes popped open. I was breathing hard, my hand was clasped across my mouth. The moon was bright and I thought it was a head looking into my window. I drew a breath, closed my eyes, then opened them again. The moon was the moon. I took a quick look around the room, then turned on the light. It was my bedroom, every corner of it known. The nightmare began to shrink away when the telephone rang. I squinted. The luminous green numbers on the clock radio showed 1:30 a.m.

I picked up the phone.

"Simone Covington," a deep voice spoke. "Let me talk to Simone Covington!"

"Yes," I mumbled.

"Forget Chloe!"

Heat rose up my neck. "Who is this?" I asked, sitting halfway up in my bed.

"Do yourself a favor . forget Chloe."

I bolted straight up. *"Who is this?"*

The voice made a wheezy laugh that sent goose bumps up my arms. "If you like breathing, stop messing in somebody else's jive!" the voice said.

I tried speaking but nothing came out. I felt sick, dizzy. I slammed the phone onto its receiver. After a few seconds, I picked it up again and dialed Cliff's number. He'd been in town for the past three days. "Cliff," I pleaded. "Come over, come over now!"

Cliff cut in. "Simone, it's two in the morning and my sleep is shifting into second gear ."

"Please, Cliff!" I begged. "A man called me and said that he's going to kill me!"

Cliff sounded a little more awake. "What?" he asked.

"Kill me!" I shouted.

There was a silence on the other end. "I'll be right over," Cliff said.

I sat, mind confused. I breathed a sigh of relief when I heard Cliff's footsteps on the stairs half an hour later. I jerked the door open. He burst into my apartment like he'd been blown through the door by the wind.

"I'm sorry, Simone," he said as I chain-locked the door, then walked into the kitchen. I must have looked bad because Cliff, who had stopped in the doorway, rushed toward me. "Baby, you all right?"

A chill raced through me. I pulled away and took a deep breath. "I need coffee," I said, opening the cabinet and reaching for the Taster's Choice.

My kitchen is a large rectangle with white and green speckled ceramic tile counters and a white tiled floor. I had hanging plants and pots next to the radio on the wide window ledge above the sink. The oak cabinets were painted white and I had talked to property management about stripping the paint and refinishing them.

"This whole thing is driving me crazy," I said, realizing that I knew no more about Chloe than the day I hit her with my car.

"Who is Chloe and why would somebody want to kill you because of her?" Cliff asked.

"You've been out of town so much," I snapped, my voice louder than I had expected, "I haven't had a chance to talk to you, tell you what's been happening!"

"Baby!" Cliff snapped. "Travel is a part of my job, you know that!"

"You don't care anymore! Somebody could kill me and you wouldn't know about it for a couple of weeks!"

"That's not true!" Cliff shouted.

"What's true," I continued, "is that your almighty job is all that you care about! I'd as soon not exist anymore!"

"Simone, you're exaggerating!"

"Call it what you want but I'm sick and tired ..." My voice trailed. I put my hand over my mouth, my strength was gone.

After a second, Cliff spoke, his voice soft and low. "I'm sorry if you feel that I've neglected you," he said.

"It's okay," I said, turning to pour two cups of hot water into the instant coffee. My body shivered. "I guess I'll have to get used to not being a priority anymore!" I said.

Cliff sighed. "Things have been crazy lately. I

guess I should've explained. I thought you'd understand, being in the business and all."

"Understand what?" I sneered. "That you're flying all over the country and ..."

Cliff was next to me. "Baby, I'm sorry," he said. "Let's not fight. Tell me everything that I've missed in the past few weeks," he said.

I took a deep breath, sipped from my coffee. I tried bringing him up to date, telling him everything, everything except that a vision, a fragment of a memory, bolted in and out of my head.

"Nothing you've told me sounds threatening," he said.

"There's one more thing. I had a friend in Vital Statistics check on Chloe. There are birth and death certificates for her."

"She's dead?"

"I've got a certificate from Columbia Bureau of Vital Statistics that says she died on _____, 19__."

"Then you're looking for the wrong girl!"

"That can't be," I said. "Martha Benton told Mama and me that she had talked to Chloe last Sunday morning."

Neither of us spoke. We were both inhaling the aroma of the coffee, thinking. "That doesn't explain how that nut got your number," he said.

I stared across the room, my mind not focused, like I couldn't trust it. "He got it from the business card I left on Martha Benton's table," I confessed. "I wrote my home phone number on the back."

"Why?"

"I wanted to talk to Chloe," I said. "Wanted to ask her about the accident, to make sure that she was okay!" It's difficult to articulate the way I felt at that moment. The odd smell came first, the image of the man's face next. A wave of terror swept over me and my kitchen took on a silence that added a weight to the moment. There was no way I could tell Cliff about this, no way I could explain that I wanted to find Chloe because I hoped she knew something that would take me back far enough to find a memory.

Cliff shot me a look. "You all right?" he asked.

"I'm tired," I said, trying to avoid looking into his eyes. I checked my watch.

Cliff looked confused, as if what I'd told him hadn't been logical. "This shouldn't be so complicated."

I shivered, not because of what he said but because of what I felt. I looked around, trying to still my fears.

"The man is going to kill Chloe!" I said.

"If he was going to kill the girl, you wouldn't have gotten the call tonight. The call was to scare you off!"

"You think so?"

"Tell me again, what did he say to you?"

"He said that he would kill me if I didn't forget Chloe," I said.

"He called her name?"

I nodded.

"The girl isn't in danger," he said.

"She's in some kind of trouble ."

"Her troubles aren't your problem. It's none of your business!"

"You can't be serious!"

"Simone, you're a rational woman. This thing can't be worth getting you killed!"

"I've got to find her!" I shouted.

"Why?"

"Her life is on the line!"

"You know that's not true!" After a few moments, Cliff took a deep breath. "Simone, will you please drop your search?"

"No!"

He sighed. I was encouraged by his look. It was calm, controlled. "Then I'd better help you," he said, his shoulders relaxing. "I don't know how I'd explain it to your folks if someone killed you!"

I nodded. I stared at my hands. "What do we do now?"

Cliff was silent, looking thoughtful. "It's no point in calling the Decatur police," he said. "They'll tell you that the call was a joke. It might be good to tell Mama's sheriff, although I can't see him doing too much about it, either."

I glanced at him, then looked away. I stood straight. Cliff stood as if he was waiting for me to say something. After a moment, I felt tears in my eyes.

"Cliff," I said, tension rippling through my body. "I'm scared."

Cliff stroked my cheek. "Don't worry, baby," he said, shifting his gaze and holding it steady. "I'm going to help you find that girl and I'm going to find the man who called you and personally put him out of commission!"

I looked beyond Cliff. So many things were unclear. I knew a man had forged Chloe and me together, but I was sure that it wasn't the man who had called. What I didn't know was why this girl had come into my life? Why was a piece of my own memory so scary?

I stared into Cliff's eyes. He wasn't a man who would step aside if trouble got in his way. Thank goodness I had him, I thought. I believed in him, believed that he would help me even though I couldn't tell him all. He tilted my head and kissed me. The chill passed. He pulled me to him, slipping his arms around me. After a moment I let my head rest on his shoulder, allowing his scent to ignite my body.

The wall phone rang. I looked at Cliff. It rang again. I groaned. My heart thudded, I stared at the instrument.

Cliff squinted. "Give it one more ring," he whispered, inching toward it. On the third ring, he picked it up and said, "Hello," his voice strong, hoarse. After a few seconds, he dropped the receiver into its cradle. His face wore disappointment. "Whoever it was hung up without talking," he said.

My heart pounded. I turned to face Cliff again. He stared at me. The caller wouldn't talk because I wasn't the person who had answered the phone, I thought.

CHAPTER NINE

A man's hand crept toward me. His skin was harsh, boils the size of small eggs grew out of his chin, his arms, the back of his hands. Yellowish pus oozed and flowed between dunes of flesh. Coarse black hair grew in oddly spaced tufts. Blood trickled from his ears and nose. And staring from the middle of all this were his evil eyes. It was as if he could read my fear.

Dear God, I thought, let this be a dream, let me be crazy, but don't let this be happening. I tried to scream but nothing came out. From someplace behind me I heard my own voice say, *"God hates cowards!"*

The words bounced through my head as the shape moved toward me, its fingers reaching for my neck.

I awakened, my hands covering my mouth, the words *God hates cowards* screaming inside my mind.

Five days later, Cliff and I were headed to South Carolina. We drove out of Atlanta, toward Augusta. It was a cold, sunny day. It had snowed the day before, but the sun had melted some of it.

The fields sparkled with an icy crust.

I looked at the sky, a clear wide expanse of blue with white fluffy clouds. The sun streamed down through the branches of the trees that lined the highway through the Savannah River Plant. I glimpsed a deer and her fawn at the edge of the woods.

A mixture of anticipation and fear settled in my stomach. I had decided to make a move. The first thing I had done was choose my weapon. I patted my purse.

A mood of solitude encircled me. I felt alone, unable to share what was going on inside of me with Mama or Cliff. Like the act of dying, the discovery of whatever it was haunted my memory demanded that I my slay own dragon! And all alone.

I thought of how Freudian my thoughts had become. The fact was that all my life I had been blessed with a lot of family support. My parents, my brothers, Uncle Ben were all people who never left me unguarded. The strength I felt today wasn't external; it lay solid and comfortable inside me, separate from the roles that tied me to the people I loved.

A few hours later, Cliff and I were sitting with Mama at her kitchen table. I had just finished telling her about the threatening phone call. "We'll go see Abe right away," she said.

"Why?" I asked.

"He may know something that can help us find out who called you," she answered.

"We should tell him everything that has happened since the accident," Cliff said.

Mama nodded.

I stood up. "Right now I'm going to the library," I said.

Mama looked interested.

"I want to check old newspaper files to see if there's something about the accident that Hester mentioned," I said.

Cliff glanced at me. "What accident?" he asked.

"A girl was hit by a car, then disappeared from the hospital sometime during the night," Mama said.

"About five, six years ago," I said.

Mama's eyes widened. "There may be a connection?"

I nodded.

Cliff grinned. "Want company?" he asked.

I shook my head. "Not this time," I said, heading for the door.

Five minutes later I was turning onto Jay Street. The Otis County library is a relatively new structure, less than fifteen years old. I noted its operating hours, then headed for Highway 601.

My third trip to where the girl had run into my car was no different than the first two. The cold sky was cloudless and paths of sunlight streaked through the trees. When I drove past Seminole Academy and Red's Barbecue, I felt a slight hesitation, but ignored it.

I got to the cabin, sat in my car and waited. Finally, I took a deep breath and stepped out of the car. Despite the cold, the earthy smell of the country side made the air come alive.

Something near my feet caught my eye. I kneeled, then grabbed a handful of hard dirt and stared at it as if it was trying to tell me something. Then I saw it, a part of the handful of dirt I'd picked up. Using the tips of my fingers, I brushed it clean.

It was a piece of silver metal with the initials of CB embossed on it. It had been a bracelet for the wrist or ankle, something that had held a chain and a clasp. I scooped away more dirt, but there was no other part of it there.

I slipped it into my purse and at the same time pulled out my weapon ... a can of mace. I stood up. My instinct told me that I was marching straight into a pit and if I had any brains at all, I'd get out of there.

I was standing on a heavy cement block of a step. The door of the cabin was old and weathered. The paint was peeling in spots. The lock looked to be just as antiquated.

Suddenly I smelled a peculiar odor. I was stepping backward toward my car when I heard the snap of a twig. Someone was there, watching me. The sound came from my left. I tried to get my breathing in order, then I turned slowly to see the man. He stood a few feet away, a young man with the build of a one-time athlete going to fat. He wore a T-shirt and jeans. The odor came from the pores of his body, his eyes held a dull expression.

My heart hammered; my body surged with adrenaline. We stared, as if each of us were trying to search the other's thoughts.

Finally, he stepped from behind the bush. "Who

are you looking for?" he asked, his speech slightly slurred.

"Chloe Benton," I said.

He stared, his face congealed, his eyes missiles peering through me. He licked his lips, shifted his body, then moved toward me.

I offered my sweetest, most reassuring smile. "Chloe Benton lives somewhere near this place," I said.

The sound of my voice stopped him. Still, he didn't say anything at all. He looked at me with bulging, hostile eyes.

"Come inside," he said.

I began breathing slowly and deeply until the tightness in my chest began to ease. I clutched my can of mace but didn't move. Nor did the wind in the surrounding woods. Everything was still, timeless.

The man's eyes held mine, watching me as if from somewhere else. Determined not to turn away, I studied him. I wanted to remember his face. Then a light wind ruffled the trees, breaking the spell.

I could tell this wasn't the reaction he had expected or wanted from me. "If you tell me more about her, maybe I'll remember her," he said, his hands motioning me toward the door.

I took a deep breath, then followed him inside, my weapon clutched between my fingers.

With the window closed, the cold air in the cabin was heavy. The man dropped in one of two straight-backed chairs that flanked the small wooden table which was in the middle of the one large room that made up the entire house. He shook a cigarette out of a pack of Camels and lit it.

A few moments passed, neither of us saying anything. I tried to think of the reason I'd followed him into the cabin, but nothing sane came to mind.

The man rocked back on the hind legs of his chair and, breaking the silence, he asked, "What's your name?"

I said nothing.

"They call me Bubba," he said.

I nodded.

"What does this girl look like that you're hunting?" he asked.

I felt my hands twitching, but gripping the can, I forced them still. I took a long, slow breath, then described how Chloe looked.

Bubba pulled on his cigarette, holding the smoke as long as he could before he blew it out. We watched it drift up to the light. Slowly he shook his head. "Nobody like that around this place," he said.

Suddenly, I had a throbbing in my head, an intoxicating smell began stinging my nostrils. For a second, I closed my eyes as the throbbing grew worse. The cabin's air filled with the scent of the cigarette. A flicker of sunlight from the window circled the smoke and cast eerie shadows.

"You all right?" Bubba asked.

My mind was having trouble working. I looked into Bubba's eyes and saw a hint of something strange. I felt a numbness, not knowing why I had come to this place.

Bubba shook another cigarette out of his pack and lit it from the butt in his mouth. His face and body were relaxed, his chin high. "You out here by yourself?" he asked, a sudden softness in his voice.

I neither moved nor spoke. I tried to shake the feeling and at the same time keep my eyes on Bubba. When he stood up, a shivering inside me started an icy path. His body was erect as he took a long, slow drag from his cigarette, holding it as long as his lungs would keep it. "I'm not going to hurt you," he said.

It was then that I realized what I felt was a buzz, the trail of smoke was from marijuana, not a cigarette. I was mad at myself; I should have been too smart for this trick. My eyes glued on him as I eased toward the door, but once I was outside, I concentrated on breathing the sweetness of the cold, fresh air.

My lungs were filled but my head was still spinning. I felt like a little girl, scared and wanting to run. Instead, I straightened up, then swallowed and forced myself to focus until my mind slipped into gear. I gripped the mace and turned to face my enemy.

Bubba was in the doorway, his eyes ringed with the darkness of gargoyles. A numbness passed through me. I was afraid to move but I reminded myself that what I felt was fear and no matter how hard the pain, I was determined to face it.

The woods were quiet.

We stared as if we were mentally circling each other, positioning ourselves for a challenge. I wouldn't move. Finally, Bubba grunted, then his hand rose and fell in a weary gesture. He stepped inside his cabin and closed the door.

I took a deep breath, then quickly walked to my car. I opened the door, sat behind the wheel staring through the windshield. I rolled my head to ease the tightness in my neck. My mind was an empty sack as I watched a small slice of sun break out from behind a cloud.

I turned on the ignition and let out a breath, then put my arms on the wheel and eased the Honda back toward the highway.

I was in front of the Coral Lodge on Tenth and Bend Street before I knew it. I had made the ten mile trip trying to convince myself that I'd taken a step in the right direction; the experience had forced me to balance my confidence with my fear.

CHAPTER TEN

The adrenaline that got me through my experience with Bubba had dispersed. I was tired. I wanted to go back to Atlanta, curl up in my bed, pull the covers over my head and forget everything that had happened since that girl ran into my car.

Chloe was hardly worth the effort, I thought, until the words *Please don't kill me!* nagged at me again and ignited that horrible feeling. I wondered if I really wanted to remember what had made me scream those words.

I drove onto Lee Street and passed the town clock. It's the street that locals call downtown, although much of the shopping takes place on the west end. The stores that remained open, that had been here since for as long as I could remember, were Stanley Drugs, Benton's Drugstore, Jesse Jewelers, the Otis Guardian Newspaper, and the Turnback clothing store.

I made a right and headed for Jackson Road.

Mama and Cliff were sitting at the kitchen table, a freshly perked pot of coffee and a plate of sandwiches before them. I sat down to eat. The bread was thinly sliced and lightly covered with mayonnaise. Ham, cheese, lettuce and tomatoes hung out of the sandwich.

No sooner was my mouth full when Mama spoke. "So, what are we going to do to get the guy who called and threatened you?" she asked.

Before I could say anything, Cliff answered. "Simone and I've talked," he said. "We haven't figured out what to do yet."

I took another bite of sandwich and tuned out what they were saying. I was tired, hungry, and my mind was going back and forth with thoughts of what I ought to do to find out what it was in my past that had pulled me so deeply into this mess.

"Find anything in the newspapers?" Mama asked in a tone that told me she knew that I wasn't listening.

After a moment, I half-nodded, half-shrugged, wondering whether or not I should tell them about my trip to the cabin, the pendant or Bubba. "I don't think ..." I started, but Cliff cut me off.

"The newspaper wasn't a good idea," he said. "You didn't have much to go on."

I considered for a moment. If I mentioned either the pendant or Bubba, Cliff would get on my case about going it alone, and I wasn't up for any of that. I decided to add both Bubba and the pendant to things to share with them whenever I felt they needed to know about it. Right now, I thought, the whole thing was just one piece of the puzzle, a puzzle that was a long way from being solved. I decided to agree with Cliff and brush the whole thing off.

"You're right," I said. "It was a long shot."

Mama frowned, her forehead wrinkled in thought. "Abe's out of town," she said, changing the subject. "He'll be back on Monday."

I glanced toward her. "Then why don't we go to Madison," I said.

Both Mama and Cliff gave me a long, serious look. Then Cliff cleared his throat.

A trip to Madison was action that I'd decided to take on my drive back from the cabin. I was going to find Chloe and, perhaps, what the similarity to her situation there was in my own life which allured me, drew me. The something so hidden I couldn't remember the details. And nothing was going to stop me. It was part of my new attitude. The words *God Hates Cowards* made me determined to go after that creep who had called me. I was going to give him the chance to do whatever he felt he was big enough to do; I wasn't going to run! I lifted my hand in a waving gesture. "I've thought it over," I said, looking Cliff in the eyes. "Martha Benton is our link to Chloe."

Cliff said nothing, but I could see from the expression on his face that the force of my words surprised him.

"I want to send Homeboy, who threatened me on the telephone, a message," I said, satisfied that I was headed in the right direction.

Cliff stared at me hard, and for a second he looked like I'd hurt his feelings.

Mama took a bite of sandwich and chewed as if she knew what my take-charge mood meant.

I held Cliff's gaze, resisting the urge to look

away. "Bait him, but this time I'll be ready!"

Cliff coughed, cleared his throat. He flinched, as if he was surprised at a suddenly pugnacious Simone. At first, I was annoyed; I was competent and capable of tracking down the sucker who had called and scared me. Then I realized Cliff and I had very little shared history; he hadn't seen me when I'd been pushed up against the wall. He didn't know that Homeboy was only a symbol, a replica of something that stirred such a terrible feeling inside me that it made me want to jump out of my skin!

The quizzical look on his face hardened, but his voice was controlled. "What are you going to do?" he asked.

I saw him, halfway, with my eyes only. My mind was somewhere else. "I'm going to tell Martha to tell Homeboy that I've got a death certificate for Chloe Ashley that says she's been dead for five years," I said.

Mama sipped from her coffee and dabbed her mouth with a napkin. The look on her face told me that she accepted my taking the offensive measure.

I folded my arms, leaning on my elbows. "I'm going to tell him that the police will be looking into her death," I said.

Cliff shifted in his seat. His stare softened and almost became blank. "You think he killed her?" he asked.

Mama gave me a thoughtful look. "He's scared," she said, and then paused to consider. "I'm sure of it."

"I am, too," I admitted.

Cliff squinted his eyes and tapped his temple with his index finger.

Mama's eyebrows arched as she threw out a new thought. "Suppose Chloe isn't dead," she said.

There was a silence, and now I felt a bit uncertain. All along I had set my mind on finding two people, the guy I dubbed Homeboy and Chloe. But, in fact, the mystery involved three people. I felt excitement bubble up. "You mean that somebody else could be buried in Chloe's grave?" I said.

Mama nodded.

"And Homeboy killed her and he's scared that if I find Chloe, somebody would want to know who the other girl is!"

Mama's eyes widened. "If you remember," she said, "Martha Benton said that Chloe is alive and that she talked to her over the phone. We have to believe that she talked to somebody, even if that somebody was not Chloe, she thought it was and she gave that person your phone number and your Homeboy was able to get it and call you." she said.

I glanced at my watch. "That's why we're going to Madison," I said. "With a little pressure, Martha Benton might tell us what we need to know to find Homeboy."

I drove 278 to 601 north and made a right. We crossed the railroad track, passed Firestone Riverside Church and the cemetery. Five miles later, we passed the cutoff to Cumberland. It took another five minutes to reach the sign, Madison Church of God. We turned right again and drove another few miles before we passed the Madison town limit.

From the moment we passed Cumberland, we saw the deepest shade of black covering a portion of the sunny sky. By the time we got to the Madison Depot Circle Road and made another right onto a badly kept dirt road, we knew that a house was on fire.

We parked near a barrier of about twenty people, then walked the half mile to the burning house where flames radiated upward, lighting up the house like a large candle. Frightened people scrambled toward the railroad track in case the fire spread and their own houses caught fire.

We joined the group that was watching the house burn and listening to the roar of the fire. A black cat streaked across my feet. I thought of something. My heart began beating fast. "Where's Martha?" I shouted.

An old woman, whose eyes showed that she hadn't realized that Martha was missing, looked past me and shook her head. I grabbed Cliff's hand and began pushing through the crowd.

"Where's Martha?" I asked a man, who motioned us toward the tracks, away from the heat. The question caught him by surprise. He touched his chin, shocked. "Where's Martha?" he began shouting, his voice carrying above the noise of the blaze and crowd.

The jolt of his words started everyone talking at the same time. The hunt for Martha Benton continued until we saw her in the window, the glow of the flames surrounding her head like a halo. The babble of voices hushed as the crowd watched Martha standing in front of the window inside the burning house.

"She'll suffocate," I screamed.

Several men tried to get near the house, but the heat was unbearable. They had to pull back. Flames squeezed through the top, bottom and sides of the house.

"Jump," the crowd shouted.

Martha looked confused. She didn't know what was happening.

"Jump," the crowd screamed.

Martha choked as billows of black smoke surrounded her. For a moment she disappeared, but then we saw her as she reached for the window. There was a large explosion, flames burst through the window, and Martha Benton's body folded like a towel.

After that, the heat became less, but the smoke increased. "She was going to jump," somebody whispered, the smell of the fire feeding every one's confusion.

Cliff and I looked at each other. If there was an odor to such things, the place would smell of frustration. I looked at Martha Benton's deflated remains and remembered the last time I had seen her. She was sitting in her house, a house sunk in shadows. Now I was sure that Homeboy had doused gasoline around her home and had struck the match that turned everything she had known into an inferno. How could a human being do what he'd done to an old woman, I wondered.

I swallowed, trying to get rid of the lump in my throat. The thought that the same Homeboy that had done this to Martha had also threatened me made me shudder. He was no amateur; he knew what he was doing. I stared off toward the railroad tracks, toward the seemingly endless pine trees. I had to find him, I thought. "He killed her," I whispered to Cliff. "Homeboy killed Martha!"

A breeze came up, enough to whip the flames and heat. I saw Cliff's eyebrow lift. "You're right," he said in a hushed voice, as if he, too couldn't believe it.

When the fire department and the police arrived, it was too late. The only thing that was left was Martha Benton's charred corpse.

CHAPTER ELEVEN

There was a dark cloud inside my head. My thoughts drifted, my mind searched. Martha Benton's death left me with a sense of loss. Homeboy had won. He'd cut off my avenue of finding Chloe, or whatever haunted my past. The surge of confidence I'd mustered seemed so childish now. I was a little girl again, ready to run, hide, and forget the whole thing.

Everything outside of me was just as gray. The air was chilly, the clouds blanketed Atlanta creating the illusion of a storm. The next few weeks found me either at the office, in my bed, in my sweat suit or getting food out of my refrigerator. Cliff tried to coax me into going with him to the Georgia Dome to see the Atlanta Falcons play the San Francisco Forty Niners, but I couldn't go anywhere other than my office or apartment. I didn't even open my mail; it was all bills anyway. I've always had a tendency to spend more money than I earn. I wasn't in the mood to assess the damages of this habit.

The more I tried to work through my despair, the more illogical it became. Flashes of some past trauma were still acute, but I had decided to live with them; it was a matter of survival. Millions of neurotics never learn the cause of their neurosis, I reasoned. Whatever had happened was buried deep in my subconscious and nothing so far had shaken it loose.

I decided to indulge in my own form of therapy cleaning my apartment. It was the way I shook things free. I dusted, vacuumed, washed dishes, and changed sheets. I had a toilet brush in my hand, watching the Comet swirl around in the bowl, when insight hit me!

I called Mama, my voice trembling with excitement. "The picture that we found in Will's photo album, where is it?" I asked.

Mama sounded surprised. "It's around here someplace," she said. "Why?"

"It's the key to this whole mess," I said.

"Simone," she said with a touch of irritation. "Make sense."

"I finally know how to find Chloe Ashley," I said, "and how to bait Homeboy out of hiding."

"I'm listening," she said.

"I don't know why I didn't think of this before,"

"Simone!" she snapped again.

"Okay. I'm going to place an announcement in the newspaper, the Otis County Guardian, and run the picture with it," I said.

"What?"

"I'm going to announce that the girl in the picture has received an inheritance, or something like that. I haven't worked out the details yet, but if Chloe is alive, we'll soon know it!"

For a minute, Mama was quiet. "I like it," she finally said.

"I'll be home on Saturday," I said.

"The Guardian goes to press on Wednesdays," she said.

"It'll take a few days to compose the thing. It'll have to wait another week. Anyway, It'll take that much time for me to work out what I'm going to say."

"I'm glad you've decided to go on looking into this thing," Mama said. "I didn't want to push you, but you seemed so determined before Martha's house caught fire."

"I've got a vested interest in getting to the bottom of this thing," I said. No sooner had the words gotten out of my mouth, than I had a flash. I was a small child, crying, pleading.

"Simone," Mama said. "You still there?"

Mama's voice made me jump. My mind was blank. The words, "I can't believe that Homeboy killed poor old Martha Benton," tumbled out of my mouth.

Mama's tone sounded like she knew something had happened. "You okay?" she asked.

"Yeah," I lied, trying to speak smoothly. "I'm fine. Like I said, Homeboy killed Martha!"

"You don't know that," she said. "The house was old, subject to catch fire anytime. Who knows, she could have dropped a match trying to light wood in that old fireplace."

"I know that I smelled gasoline at that fire. I'll give you two-to-one that Homeboy decided the best way to get rid of me was to get rid of

Martha!" I said.

"Abe has written it off as an accident," she said.

"I don't care," I snapped, remembering the feeling of helplessness I'd just experienced. "I'm going after Homeboy for other reasons."

"I guess you haven't gotten any more phone calls, any more threats," she said.

"Homeboy probably figured that once Martha was dead, I'd forget about Chloe and, you know, he was almost right."

"When you put that announcement in the paper, he'll be after you again," she said.

"I'll change my number, get an unlisted one."

"A good idea," Mama said.

"And," I continued, "I'll set up a number with an answering service and get them to answer in a way that they will get a number from him."

"Sounds good to me," she said.

So many ideas began swirling in my head, I had to stop talking to Mama and write them down. "Talk to you later," I said, "got a million things to work out."

I felt fired up. I grabbed a pad and scribbled out a draft of the announcement. Then I checked the phone number of the answering service. I used the same one Sidney used. Finally, the sheriff crossed my mind. We'd get him in on this, I thought. Have him waiting to grab Homeboy! I was energized.

The next thing I did was call Cliff. "You won't believe what's happened," I said.

"You won the lottery?" he asked.

"What?"

"Sounds like you've hit the jackpot," he said.

"I've done better," I said.

"I'll bring the wine," he said.

"For what?"

"The celebration!"

I did a quick dance, complete with butt wiggles. It's my usual mature way of celebrating my wins. I stripped off my sweat suit, took a hot shower, and then got dressed, put on makeup with dabs of Seduction, Cliff's favorite perfume.

It was ten of eight when Cliff arrived at my apartment door. He pulled me into his arms, his solid body warm. I felt his hands on my back, strong, pressing me into him.

There was the hint of Canoe scent, and while he kissed me, I tasted wine in his mouth. I pulled away and led him to the leather sofa next to the coffee table. His brown coat was opened, he wore no tie. His eyes were very calm, very direct. He pulled me to him and kissed me again, but this time I pulled away, and before he had a chance to do anything, I held out the pad that I'd used to jot down my ideas.

The corner of his mouth tilted; he was irritated. He glanced at my notes, frowned, then handed it back.

"What's this?" he asked.

I glanced at him, anxious for his cooperation.

"It's my plan," I said. He listened as I detailed what action I was going to take to track down Chloe and Homeboy.

Cliff wasn't in the mood for what I was offering. "What charges will the good sheriff hold

Homeboy on when he grabs him?" he asked once I'd finished my summary.

I stirred uncomfortably. "Charges?"

Cliff cleared his throat with a skeptical hum. "He may question Homeboy but you know that he can't hold him without any charges," he said.

"I hadn't thought of that," I admitted.

Cliff's expression was impatient. He gestured carelessly. "You of all people should have," he said.

"Let me think," I said. A word flashed through my head.

"Kidnapping," I blurted.

Cliff stared at me blankly. "What?"

I tossed the notepad on the coffee table. "He kidnapped the girl from the hospital, remember? And he held a gun on the nurse and doctor. I bet the sheriff can get enough out of that to put him away for a while!"

Cliff hunched his shoulders. He broke off eye contact, shaking his head in frustration.

"I'll see that Sheriff Abe gets a warrant and ..."

He stood up. He stuck his hands in his pockets and strolled over to the window. "Suppose your Homeboy isn't the same person who snatched the girl from the hospital?" he asked.

Here was another shift in perspective. I realized Bubba wasn't the black guy with the short Afro that witnesses had described as the one who had snatched Chloe from Otis General Hospital. Even though I had found the pendant outside his cabin, his voice wasn't the one that had called me in the middle of the night. Cliff's insights were making me frustrated. "Why are you trying to trip me up?" I snapped.

Cliff crossed his arms, his tone sounded almost as exasperated. "I'm trying to help. I know you don't see any connection, but as a lawyer, I lean toward the legal!"

"I know the law as good as you do," I snapped. "And I'll tie all the loose knots before I'm finished, you'll see!" I said. I wouldn't ask him, but he made me wonder how Bubba fitted into the puzzle. It could mean that there were four people involved; four people could be responsible for killing the person in Chloe's grave. I took a deep breath and tried to soften my tone. "If I remember, there were witnesses at the hospital who gave the sheriff a pretty good description of the guy who kidnapped Chloe. I think it might be a good idea to get the details of that incident so I can have it in place when I need it," I said.

Cliff was staring out of the window. "Good!" he snapped.

"Okay. The picture, the announcement, the answering service, and the warrant, anything else?"

Cliff hesitated, then turned to look me in the eyes. He smiled, a look mixed with expectancy creased his face.

"Apprehension?" he asked.

I stirred but didn't break eye contact.

"I liked you better when you were so scared that you wanted my help," he said.

CHAPTER TWELVE

Rain drops began to dot the windshield as we hit I-20. By the time we drove across the South Carolina state line, the rain was a steady patter.

Four hours later, we walked into Mama's kitchen. The scent of baking, a rich combination of vanilla and chocolate, blended. Mama was easing a blade through a pan of brownies, making parallel cuts. She was wearing a navy and white pantsuit; her silky mixed gray hair reminded me of how beautifully she was aging.

We sat at the table across from one another, the pan of brownies between us. The top was light brown. Mama's knife had left a ragged line, a portion of brownie jutting up through the broken crust. Just under the surface, the texture was as dark and moist as soil. There were walnuts and small clusters of chocolate chips. Mama lifted out the first square with a spatula and passed it to me.

I poured us each a cup of coffee. My mouth was filled with warm chocolate. The taste made me moan with enjoyment.

"What did you come up with?" Mama asked.

"A master plan," Cliff answered. "Simone needs

to get a copy of the report from the sheriff on that man who kidnapped Chloe from the hospital."

"I'll get Abe on the phone today," Mama said.

"Show your mother the announcement," Cliff urged.

I reached into my handbag and pulled the sheet of white paper from it, then read aloud what I'd written:

Notice: Sidney Jacoby, Esq., attorney for the estate of Samuel Benton, is seeking the whereabouts of the young woman in this photograph. She is the only living relative of the deceased who was a native of Allen County, South Carolina. There is an estate of $75,000. Anybody knowing her whereabouts should call (404) 123-1234. A reward is offered.

Mama listened; Cliff ate a section of the brownies that was in the shape of Florida.

"Do you think its right to say those things if they aren't true?" Mama asked when I'd finished reading.

"It's the only way," I said.

"Is there a law against making that kind of announcement if it isn't true?" she asked.

"There's no law," Cliff said, his mouth half full. "If Chloe is alive, she might sue Simone for publishing a false claim."

I sat forward. "Once Homeboy is in jail, I'll repent from my lying ways and publish an explanation," I said. "I've got a hunch, though, that when I show Chloe her own death certificate, she won't want to sue!"

The telephone rang. Mama got up to answer it. "Fingers has been shot," she said. She put her palm across the mouthpiece so the other party couldn't hear her talk. "He's in intensive care."

It took us about fifteen minutes to reach the hospital. The rain was steady with clouds the color of galvanized pipes. It reminded me of the day I'd hit Chloe; the gray rainy skies had looked the same way.

Hester was in the emergency room with its pale green walls. Two nurses were struggling to hold onto her arms. She was swinging wildly at them. One of them said, "Just relax. Everything's going to be fine."

"Fingers!" Hester cried before the sedative took hold. One of the nurses hooked a tube into her arm, then left the room. We stood listening to the sound of her breathing. While it was slow and steady, there was a terseness about her body, as if she knew that something was happening.

Sheriff Abe appeared suddenly in the doorway, motioning us to follow him into the hall.

We looked at him in shock. "What happened?" Mama asked.

"Bozie Jackson shot the boy," he said.

Bozie Jackson was one of Hester's neighbors. He was a man about seventy, fond of guns, and suspicious of light-fingered boys.

We stared at Abe, expecting him to say something more. He wiped at his nose with his hand. "He said he heard a noise in the back of his house," Abe continued. "He got his gun and went to investigate. He found Fingers trying to steal."

Cliff looked skeptical. "Did he have to shoot the boy?" he asked.

Sheriff Abe's eyes had a hint of perplexity, his eyes opening wide as if trying to focus better, his eyebrows rising slightly. He turned away from us and stared off down the corridor. "Bozie said the boy tried to attack him," Abe said. "Said he shot him in self-defense."

Mama shook her head in disbelief. "That's crazy," she snapped. "Fingers was a thief but he wouldn't hurt anybody, much less an old man."

Abe glanced back towards Mama, his eyes showing that he agreed. "I hear you," he said, "but until the boy pulls through, we'll have to take Bozie's word for what happened."

Mama sighed, as if in disgust. When she spoke again, her voice rose a step. She was angry. "This is going to kill Hester!" she said.

Sheriff Abe shook his head sadly, staring into Mama's eyes. "The boy was all she had," he said, "all she wanted!"

When Hester's eyes finally opened, we were there. Mama took Hester's hand and smiled. "You had us worried," she said.

"Fingers?" Hester asked.

"We don't know yet," Mama said. "He's out of surgery, but the next few hours will be touch and go."

Hester just looked at us. Mama gripped her hand, holding on with all her strength. Hester made no effort to pull away, nor did she say anything. She closed her eyes and looked as if something terrible, something deadly was flowing through her.

I prayed that Fingers would live; it was the only

hope for Hester's sanity. Fingers *was* all she had.

"Candi," Hester's voice choked itself off. Her hand was still in Mama's grip. Leaning against the hospital bed, she rocked gently. The bed swayed to her mournful rhythm. Sweat ran down Hester's face, mixing with tears, then she seemed to start suffocating, her breath stifled.

I reached across to another bed and grabbed two pillows which I used to bolster Hester's head. Hester sucked air until her breathing was quiet again.

Hours later, a doctor came to explain things. He was the same plump-faced man who'd taken care of Chloe. "Your son is alive," he said, looking directly into Hester's eyes.

She peered at him through eyes surrounded by tear-swollen flesh.

"By all odds he should have died on the spot," said the doctor. "When he came in, he had no blood pressure. He'd been shot twice. One bullet glanced his forehead and skull. The other went through the soft tissue of his face and came out of his neck. Either bullet could have finished him if it had gone just a hairbreadth in another direction."

"Is he going to live?" Mama asked.

The doctor smiled. "We don't know," he said softly, his eyes directed on Hester. "We'll have to wait another twenty-four hours."

The next morning Hester was allowed to see Fingers, and because of her own fragile state, the doctor allowed both me and Mama to go into the room with her.

Fingers was lying in a bed. He looked so small beneath the covers, like a dead squirrel. His body was perfectly still. There were tubes everywhere, draped over the bed rail, trailing out haphazardly across the floor. Fingers was stuck full of them, like a puppet on a set of strings.

The room was filled with gray light. We walked to Fingers' bed.

There was an orderly on the other side, a very short dark-haired young man, working at the tubes. He ignored us. A large box-like machine with a tiny yellow video screen sat on a cart behind him, beeping steadily.

The orderly was wearing translucent rubber gloves. Through them I could see the hair on the back of his hands.

In a few minutes, the doctor entered the room. "You can only stay a minute," he said. Then he turned to the orderly and they whispered back and forth. While they talked, the doctor scribbled on his clipboard.

I watched Hester closely. She took a deep breath, then took her son's hand. Fingers' eyes flickered at the pressure. When they opened a second later, they fell right on her. Then they didn't move at all. A set of tubes were stuck up his nose. His forehead was beaded with sweat.

Fingers stared at his mother for a second, and then his lips moved, as if by reflex, into a smile. It wasn't a normal smile; it was unlike any I'd ever seen before. His lips stretched out straight across to either side of his face so that he looked like a dog baring his teeth. His eyes didn't move at all.

"I'm here," Hester whispered. "I'm right here!"

I turned away as Fingers seemed to try to respond but couldn't. When, suddenly, he made a harsh, gasping sound at the back of his throat, the machine's beeping increased in tempo, I looked back. The doctor and the orderly glanced up from their discussion.

Fingers shut his eyes. The beeping gradually slowed back down.

Hester held her son's hand for another minute or so, until the doctor asked us to leave.

Though the doctor suggested we go home and get some rest, we all stayed at the hospital. I was glad that Cliff was with us. Every few hours, he'd go out and get food, then coerce us into eating.

Fingers drifted in and out of consciousness, the periods between each state lasting no more than a minute or two, and sometimes just a second. Hester wasn't allowed to see him again.

Hours later, two doctors, an orderly and a nurse walked toward us. When I recognized Dr. Reed, I knew what he was going to say. The four of us waited, tense, as if it was going to be a surprise.

Dr. Reed's eyes were dark, cautious. "He's dead," he whispered.

I groaned. The orderly, who had walked up behind Hester, caught her as she collapsed.

CHAPTER THIRTEEN

The chasm between the highs of life and the lows of death is boredom. I like it, it's dependable, stable, and gives the delusion of eternity.

I thought about poor Fingers and bit my lip. I felt my eyes water. The whole thing was almost too much. The words *run and hide* bolted through my mind. For Fingers I hated life and I hated death. More than that, I hated that the poor kid hadn't been given the chance to choose between the two.

The minute we stepped outside the hospital, the wind seemed to pick up. The air was cold and fresh. Cliff, who seemed to sense my feelings, put a guiding hand on my elbow. I reached and grabbed Mama's hand as the three of us walked toward my Honda.

It was a little after midnight when we got to my parents' house. My father, who had visited the hospital three or four times during the course of events, was in the kitchen. He sat at the table, a fresh pot of coffee had just been brewed.

"He's dead!" Mama said as we walked into the room.

Daddy cleared his throat. "I know," he said as he stood to pour coffee for each of us. "I got a call from Gertrude. She's on duty tonight."

Daddy's cousin Gertrude had worked as a nurses' aide at the hospital for ten years. She liked her job because she's the first to know of a tragedy; the first to notify everybody of family members' illnesses and infirmities.

I was tired and discouraged. I sipped my coffee and stared at the copy of the newspaper announcement that I'd written. I thought about Chloe, wondered whether it was worth looking for Homeboy. Suppose she's already dead, suppose ... my mind swung back to Fingers and Martha Benton. Their downfall was somebody's perception of them. I thought again of Chloe, remembered her face, her fear.

I sighed. I was tired, my thoughts were a mixture of mumbo jumbo. Maybe time and life will catch up with Homeboy, I thought, when the words *please don't kill me!* made its sprint through my mind. This time, instead of seeing the man's face, I saw Fingers, and felt his panic as if he was running to escape death. Whatever the expression on my face, it got Cliff's attention. He came over and sat in a chair beside me. "You all right?" he asked, touching my hand.

"Yes ... no ... I mean, I'm tired," I said, trying to shake off the nausea of the image. I took a deep breath, then hauled my handbag onto the table and fumbled in the front pocket for an aspirin. What I found was the pendant with the initials CB that I'd picked up at the cabin. "I forgot about this," I said, holding it up for everybody to see.

Daddy looked over at me and frowned. Cliff looked puzzled, but Mama peered at the small piece of jewelry with interest.

I thought for a moment and decided it was time to confess. "I found it when I went to the cabin the other week," I said.

Cliff gestured his irritation. This time, Daddy looked puzzled. Mama, who seemed to always look cool and relaxed, smiled knowingly.

"When I told you that I was going to the library, I went to the cabin."

"Alone!" Cliff hollered.

I folded my hands in front of me. "I met a man out there. He said his name was Bubba."

Cliff took a deep breath, then let it out slowly like he was trying to be patient with me. "Why do you insist on doing these things alone?"

I blinked. Cliff's words added to my acid indigestion.

"I suppose you would have said something sooner if he had been the man you're setting your little trap for!" he sneered.

I rolled my eyes and pointed at the announcement. "If Bubba was Homeboy, this whole thing would be useless!" I snapped.

Mama glanced at me, then spoke, her voice neutral. "What happened out there?" she asked. I studied her profile and wondered whether she suspected what was going on inside my head. She gave me that look, the one that made me feel that she not only knew what I'd done but the reason I'd done it.

I slumped down in my chair, breathed deeply and tried to shake off the pressure to spill my guts. "Nothing. Oh yeah, the place smelled funny." I paused for effect. "It turned out that I got a buzz from the weed that Bubba was smoking," I said.

Mama was not shocked, but my very protective father's mouth flew open and he stared at me. Cliff's countenance changed immediately. He tried to smother a grin.

"I got in the fresh air in time," I said, avoiding my father's eyes.

Mama seemed intrigued by my find. She reached out her hand. "The pendant?" she asked.

I handed it over. "I found it outside the cabin door, on the ground. It's my bet that it belongs to my girl," I said.

"Did you see anything else to make you believe that?" Mama asked.

I shook my head wearily. "If you mean did I search the place, the answer is no. I had to get out of there what with Bubba's trying to get me high."

Mama looked thoughtful. "Did you know Bubba? I mean, have you seen him around town before?" she asked.

I yawned. "I don't know him personally, but I got the impression that he might be some kin to those Terrys from out behind Furman."

"We should print a copy of this pendant with the announcement, too," she said.

"I'm dead tired," I said, looking at Mama. "You're going to be busy taking care of Hester all next week, aren't you?" I asked.

Mama sipped her coffee, her eyes glued on the pendant. "I'll have time to put the announcement in the paper, if that's what you mean," she said.

I kicked off my shoes, then looked at my watch. We had been talking for over an hour. "I'll come home for Fingers' funeral," I said, thinking again of how scared he must have been when that old man pointed a gun at him and pulled the trigger.

Cliff seemed to be reading my mind. "I don't think that old man had to shoot the boy," he said.

Daddy shook his head. "Fingers wouldn't hurt Bozie," he said. "The black community isn't going to buy his story."

I opened my eyes and sat straight up. "You think there's going to be trouble?" I asked.

Mama, whose eyes stayed glued to the pendant, shook her head. "I'm going to talk to Abe again," she said. "Try to avoid any confrontation."

"Bozie is half blind," I said. "He could have thought ..."

Daddy cut in. "Bozie has known Fingers all his life," he said. "He knew good and well that Fingers wouldn't hurt him!"

Mama cleared her throat. "Now, James," she said, "no use starting a commotion over Fingers. It won't bring him back!"

"It'll keep our other black boys from being shot by half-cocked old men," he snapped.

"Fingers wouldn't have gotten shot if he hadn't been in Bozie's house," she said.

"It would be a nightmare if the blacks and whites start fighting over this thing," I said.

"There's no need for a fight!" Mama snapped.

"Sidney had a case like that," I said. "You remember, Mama, you helped me with it."

For a moment, she looked puzzled.

"The Thomas Matthews case," I said.

Mama nodded.

"What happened?" Cliff asked.

"A burglar, Steven Foster, tried to break into the home of our client, Thomas Matthews. Thomas Matthews shot and killed him. The DA's office pressed charges against our client alleging that Steven Foster didn't have a weapon so he posed no threat to Thomas Matthews or his wife."

"How did Sidney defend his client?" Cliff asked.

"Well, both Thomas Matthews and his wife swore that Steven Foster had a gun, so Sidney assigned me to find it."

"And we did find it," Mama said, smiling. "The Matthews' obedient school trained dog had picked it up and hid it under their couch." She smiled. "I remember the look on Mrs. Matthews' face."

"It might be a good idea to ask Abe to look around Bozie's house to see if he finds something that might have scared Bozie into thinking that Fingers was going to hurt him."

Mama nodded, but Daddy was skeptical. "Fingers wouldn't do anything to that old man!" he growled. "Bozie was probably carrying a grudge and ..."

"James," Mama interrupted. "If Fingers scared Bozie, it's understandable that he shot him!"

Daddy sounded mad. "You siding against your

kinfolk?" he asked.

"I'm siding with the truth," Mama said. "It's the right thing, and the right thing is the only thing to do!"

"The black folks don't take too kindly to their boys being killed," Daddy said. "Folks will want Bozie checked out!"

Mama sighed and I could see that she too was tired. "I'll see that Abe looks into it," she whispered.

Nobody said another word. The conversation was over. The pain of exhaustion had overcome all four of us. I looked at my watch again, then picked up my shoes. "It's after one-thirty," I said, standing up. "I'm going to bed!"

Cliff yawned and nodded.

Mama looked at the empty cups on the table. "One thing more," she said as an afterthought. "It might be a good idea for all of us to look at that cabin again."

Cliff was in the middle of another yawn, but he smothered it so he could beat me to the punch. "This time we'll do it together!" he said, before I had a chance to say anything.

Mama sipped the last of her cold coffee and stared at the pendant. She shook her head, mystified. "This is a pretty expensive piece of jewelry," she said, her voice sounding odd. I could feel caution flashing in me like a yellow traffic light. I looked at her but said nothing. Instead, I turned and headed for the door.

CHAPTER FOURTEEN

Three weeks later, we got our phone call. The announcement had run twice. The call wasn't from Chloe or Homeboy; it was from a Mr. Clyde Collier who lived in Benford, South Carolina.

At 2:30 p.m. the next Saturday afternoon, Cliff, Mama and I left Otis. The afternoon light had the gray look of twilight and the air was chilly. We drove Highway 278 out of Foster to 68, which took us into York. From there we crossed the railroad track and drove into Bedford County.

Mr. Collier lived just south of Hilton Head Island, a tropical sanctuary for the rich. His house was large, built of board and with a steeply pitched shingled roof and a large front porch that circled both front and the right side. The exterior was blue, the trim painted white. Wood frame windows formed the upper portion of the walls on all sides.

Mr. Collier was white; he was narrow through the face with black, unruly eyebrows and short-cropped salt-and-pepper hair. He looked like he'd lived his life in a business suit. Today, he wore dark, stiff jeans and a new plaid flannel shirt, packing creases still showing, two buttons open to expose a portion of his white undershirt.

We followed him into his house. The room we entered was warmed by a fireplace. It was overly decorated, filled with objects collected from foreign ports. There was a stack of newspapers on the floor beside a black leather wing chair, a smaller pile of papers on an ottoman, and magazines on the end table. There was a table on which there was a typewriter, next to a stack of books.

Mr. Collier waved us toward the chairs. "Would you like some coffee?" he asked.

"Thanks, but we're fine," Mama said.

Mr. Collier looked hard at us. "I don't understand," he said, pointing at the newspaper article. My announcement had been cut out. "I spotted this in the Otis Guardian two weeks ago," he said.

"We're looking for that girl," I said.

He shifted in his chair. "Why?"

"The inheritance ."

He interrupted. "The only inheritance my daughter will get will be from me!"

"The girl in that picture, Chloe Ashley, is she your daughter?" I asked.

He smiled. "That girl is my daughter, but her name isn't Chloe Ashley," he said.

Nobody said a word. The impact of his statement hit hard. "Are you sure?" Mama asked.

He nodded. "Those pictures over there," he pointed to the mantle above the fireplace, "are pictures of my daughter. Take a look."

The three of us got up and walked over to the fireplace. For a moment, nothing was said. Our

picture of who we thought to be Chloe Ashley
looked very much like the girl who stared back at
us. There were pictures of a girl from six to sixteen.

"What is your daughter's name?" Mama asked.

"Sarah Turner," he said. "And she's no kin to a
Samuel Benton of Allen." He grinned. "Really, I
don't know what you all are up to, but before I
called you, I checked and there ain't no such person as Samuel Benton of Allen County."

I took a deep breath. "I made that up," I confessed.

"For heaven's sake, why?" he asked.

"A few months ago I had an accident," I began.
"The girl in that picture ran out in front of me in
the rain and I struck her, my automobile did, that
is. We took her to Otis Hospital for treatment. A
few days later, a man kidnapped her out of the
hospital. I wrote the announcement in an effort to
find her," I explained.

"You sure you know what you're talking
about?"

"Why do you ask?".

"When did you hit her?" he asked.

"Three months ago."

He frowned. "I ain't heard from Sarah in about
three months," he said.

"Are you worried?"

He shook his head. "You must understand," he
said. "Sarah and I have a strange kind of relation-
ship."

Mama smiled, the kind of smile that seemed to
hypnotize people into spilling their guts.

Mr. Collier continued. "I hope you don't judge me too harshly," he began, the depth of the sadness in his voice seemed to affect its pitch. He looked in the direction of the pictures. "When I was a young man, I fell in love with the prettiest woman you'd ever seen. Her eyes were clear, sparkling, and she had a sweetness of a magnolia in full bloom. I couldn't marry that woman, but I never wanted another for my wife."

I shifted in my chair.

"I suspect you've guessed by now that Sarah's mama was a black woman," he said, "a very fine black woman."

We nodded knowingly. It was the only explanation for the pictures of the child that hung above Mr. Collier's fireplace.

He began fiddling with his ring. "Sara's mama was an educated woman. We didn't mean for things to turn out the way they did ... didn't mean for Sarah to come, but it happened and Sarah's mama, being the fine woman that she was, consented to raise Sarah by herself."

"Sarah didn't know you were her father?" I asked.

Mr. Collier seemed as if he didn't hear me. "I wasn't the man I am now," he said, as if talking to himself. "I guess I wasn't much of a man at all."

Nobody said a word. For a few minutes, Mr. Collier seemed to be in his own private thoughts, seeking the answers from someplace inside himself.

"That was a long time ago," Mama said.

When Mr. Collier's eyes turned back to us, they

were filled with tears. "I'm a believer in doing the right thing," he said. "I loved Sarah's mama, loved Sarah, too, but I couldn't take them with me. At that time, it just wasn't proper." He shook his head apologetically. "I took care of them, though, saw that they had everything they needed. Sarah's sweet mama understood. She didn't make demands." He cleared his throat. "She wrote me letters, sent me pictures, made sure I knew everything about Sarah. She did that until the good Lord took her away."

I glanced toward the photos again and wondered what that child had thought when she found out that her benevolent benefactor was her white father.

"It's a shame," he said, looking past me toward the pictures on the fireplace. "Now that I'm retired, I sit alone, my thoughts drifting. Nobody calls, writes, or comes over to visit. Sometimes I open my old letters. Most of the time I read--newspapers, books ." His voice trailed.

When Mama spoke, her voice was soft, gentle. "How old was Sarah when her mama died?" she asked.

"Sixteen," he said. "I hadn't seen Sarah or her mama for years, though I got letters regularly. Anyhow, right before she died, I got a letter asking that I take care of Sarah, make sure she got a proper education and all. I wrote back my promise. Her mama died six months later. I found a boarding school for Sarah, a school in New England. Sarah stayed there until she finished."

"You never visited?" I asked.

He shook his head. "I paid all of Sarah's bills, sent her an allowance. She didn't need for anything!"

Mama smiled, as if she understood what this man had tried to do, but I knew that look was a ploy. knew how she hated my father's pushing my brothers into a military career and how she argued that he was sacrificing her children to an institution, an institution that couldn't care for them the way she could.

Mr. Collier spoke in a whisper, as if he was letting us in on a secret. "Sarah did well. She finished school summa cum laud in her class. I was in the audience that day, you know, for her mama. She would have been proud of our daughter."

We smiled, but nobody spoke for nearly a minute after that.

"You understand, I did what I could," he said as if he was trying to convince himself that what had happened was beyond his control.

I took a deep breath. I had mixed emotions about what he was telling us.

"Does Sarah know you're her father?" Mama asked.

He nodded. "Sure does," he said, a noticeable relief in his voice. "When I retired, I decided to find Sarah and tell her that I was her daddy; that I was the man who had taken care of her and her mama."

"When?" Mama asked.

"Five, six years ago," he said. "Sarah came to see me, we talked."

"How did she take it?" Mama asked.

"She was a tad bit angry at first, but she'd grown up to be a fine young woman, properly educated, somebody her mama would have been proud of. We talked and, well, all in all, I think we hit it off pretty good."

"Sarah visits often?" Mama asked.

He shook his head. "Sad to say, I ain't seen her but that one time."

"What kind of young woman was she then?" I asked.

"What do you mean?" he asked.

"Did she act like she was scared?" I asked.

Mr. Collier shook his head. "If I remember correctly, she didn't talk too much."

"So you haven't heard from her in five, six years?" Mama repeated.

"Sarah calls a few times a year, lets me know things are all right. She's working, says she can't get back this way."

We sat in silence. I picked up the newspaper announcement and wondered what to do next. I was beginning to feel that I'd hit another dead end. Clyde Collier and Sarah Turner were one more piece of the puzzle. What I needed was to brainstorm with Mama. We'd talk about everything, everything but the strange pungent smell and the image of an unknown man I'd seen in Chloe's eyes.

"What about *money*?" Cliff asked, his words instinctive out of his profession. Mr. Collier shrugged. When he spoke, his voice was quiet, even. "What about the money?" he asked.

"You send Sarah money?"

"Sure do," Mr. Collier said without the slightest hesitation. Sarah's all I got in this world. Did I tell you that I set up a trust for her when she was born? It did quite well!"

"A trust fund?" Mama asked.

He nodded. "In three months, my little girl will be a rich woman, a half million dollars rich!"

I swallowed.

"Sarah knows about the fund?" Mama asked.

"Sure does," Mr. Collier beamed. "I gave her all the particulars when she visited me that time, five, six years ago."

CHAPTER FIFTEEN

The light of the full moon shone brightly through a cloudless sky. Except for the occasional breeze that rattled the car, everything was quiet. The drive from Benford seemed long because none of us hardly said a word, deep in our own thoughts.

It was after midnight when we finally got to Otis, and I pulled into my parents' driveway. I felt myself shiver as we got out of the car, a combination of the cold air and the confusion from what we'd learned in Benford.

The house was dark except for a single light that burned in the kitchen. We opened the door quietly, not wanting to wake my father.

Cliff walked to the kitchen table and I headed for the refrigerator where I pulled out what remained of the fruit salad we'd had earlier. Mama went straight to the coffee pot to fill it first with filtered water then hazelnut coffee.

"I can't believe that Chloe and Sarah Turner are the same women," I said.

Mama flipped the switch of the coffee maker. "They can't be," she said, her tone not one of amusement. To her it was a given fact.

Cliff leaned forward in his chair and picked up his fork. "They look the same to me," he said before he filled his mouth with fruit.

"That's why I borrowed the picture of Sarah from Mr. Collier," Mama said.

"It's ironic that Chloe didn't know her mother until five years ago and ..."

Cliff cut in. "Sarah Turner didn't know her father until that time, either," he said.

Mama reached in the cabinet and pulled out three mugs. The aroma of the coffee filled the room. "We've found something that they had in common," she said. "Something that might be the solution we're looking for."

I was puzzled. "What?" I asked.

"You've got a death certificate. Chloe Ashley is dead, right?"

Cliff, whose right eyebrow arched, cut in again. "That means the girl you hit, the girl who we're looking for, is Sarah Turner and not Chloe Ashley," he said.

Mama paused. "Or," she said in a triumphant tone, "she may be Chloe Ashley pretending to be Sarah Turner!"

I stood looking at Mama, who stared back. I started to speak, then changed my mind and said nothing as her words sank in.

"I thought about this in the car," she said, and then paused to consider. "Suppose Sarah Turner and Chloe Ashley met in that school up north and became friends. They had a lot in common.both had an unknown parent, both came from South

Carolina, and they looked alike."

I cleared my throat. "We'd have to assume that they look like identical twins," I said, "and that's jumping to a pretty big conclusion!"

Mama ignored my tone and poured coffee. "Suppose they found their missing parent around the same time and decided to come for a visit. Sarah Turner visits her father; Chloe Benton visits her mother."

I studied her. "Okay," I said.

"And," Cliff picked up, "Sarah Turner learned of her trust fund, told Chloe how she would inherit half a million dollars in five years."

Mama nodded. "Then there is an accident. Hank James," she said.

"The girl who Hester told us was snatched from the hospital in the middle of the night," I said.

"If that girl was Sarah Turner, then Chloe and whoever is in this with her might have decided that if Sarah died, the trust fund would die with her."

"Somebody, maybe the guy who had married Chloe, decided to snatch Sarah from the hospital."

"When she died, they gave her Chloe's identity and Chloe took Sarah's," Mama said.

I was silent. "That's why she didn't want us to know her name. They're after the money," I said.

Mama's brow knitted. "And in three months, it'll all be over. They'll have half a million dollars and nobody would have been the wiser!"

Although Mama's assumption sounded logical, I thought of something else. "That girl was running scared when I hit her!" I said. "Chloe was running for her life. I saw her, talked to her, looked into her eyes, and I saw fear!"

Mama made a slight face but when she spoke, her voice was soft. "What did she say to you, Simone?"

I took a deep breath and closed my eyes, forcing myself to concentrate. When I opened them, I replied, "'This ain't nothing like what's going to happen to me if I don't get away from this place,'" I said, making quote marks with my fingers.

Mama's look was warm, relaxed. "That doesn't sound like she was running from a person to me," she said quietly.

I bit my lip, trying to force detached emotions, but the feeling of pity, then the man's image intruded on my thoughts. My pulse quickened; I straightened in my chair. This time, I could feel a message trying to rise to the surface. Something linked the girl, the image and me together, but what? I thought it had been our shared fear. If I was wrong, then I had something else to find. Why had I transferred my struggle onto this stranger? It was an answer I had to track alone, but it had an uneasiness connected to it. I tried setting the idea aside, but I knew that it was going to stick with me until I found Chloe Ashley or Sarah Turner, whichever was the girl I'd hit with my car.

Cliff, who had propped his elbows on the table and made a steeple of his fingers, cleared his throat as if he'd seen something peculiar about my expression. "You all right?" he asked, as he studied my face.

I didn't answer.

"I've seen that look before and I don't like it. What's the matter with you?" he asked again.

I fought to manage my feelings. "I'm fine," I said, as I spread my hand, "really, I'm okay."

Mama frowned. "Something is wrong.what is it?" she asked.

I took a deep breath and exhaled. "I'm okay, honest," I said, grateful that my anxiety was beginning to subside. I waved Mama to continue. "What were you saying?"

Cliff's expression was worried for a moment, then it changed. He smiled. "That guy who called you and told you to forget Chloe Ashley . he was trying to scare you off," he said. When Cliff smiled, it was more with his eyes than his lips. "He had no intention of hurting you!"

Mama's slightly troubled expression vanished when Cliff began speaking.Now her eyes shined, the way they did when she knew she was on the right track. "I guess they didn't like Simone locating Martha and asking questions about Chloe," she said. Something in her voice made me feel that she wasn't satisfied that everything was fine with me, but she moved on with her theory. "They've waited five years for half a million dollars," she said.

I felt some misgivings, but pushed them aside and made myself concentrate on what Mama was saying. "That doesn't explain why the girl was running when I hit her," I said, trying to look Mama in the eyes. "You told me that she ran into my car, remember. That proves that she was running from something, somebody!"

Mama half-smiled. "She did look like she was running to me, but I can't figure out why."

"We'll ask her when we find her," Cliff said.

I still felt confused. "Nothing you've said so far explains why Martha was killed," I said.

"We don't know that Martha was murdered, but if she was, maybe she began asking questions, maybe she insisted that Chloe come for a visit and ..." she paused, "maybe it was an accident after all."

I shook my head. "I told you I smelled gasoline at that fire, gasoline that somebody poured before it was set!"

Mama sighed. "If it'll make you feel better, I'll get Abe's report," she said. "Let you see his conclusions about Martha's death."

I said nothing.

Mama went on. "Back to Chloe Ashley, impersonator of Sarah Turner. For five years they've been hiding out, and from time to time she called both Clyde Collier and Martha Benton," she said.

"Why?" I asked.

Mama raised her shoulders.

"Why would she call Martha?" I asked. "I can see her keeping in touch with Clyde, the money and all, but why keep in touch with Martha?"

Mama cocked her head. "Martha was Chloe's mother, a mother she'd found after years of separation. She probably wanted to keep in touch."

I opened my mouth to say something but Cliff raised his hand to interrupt. "Miss Candi, everything you say sounds possible to me except for one thing. Let me look at those pictures again," he said, holding his hand out.

Mama opened her purse, took out the pictures and put both in Cliff's hand. He examined the pictures thoughtfully, giving each one his undivided attention before he laid it on the table. Finally, he shrugged apologetically. "I understand where you're coming from, Miss Candi, but they look like the same girl to me," he said, placing each picture on the table.

I reached for the pictures and studied them briefly. I refused to look too hard. I couldn't chance the flash of the image or the knot in my stomach that accompanied it. The girl we'd named Chloe Ashley looked about twenty when her picture was taken; the other girl looked about sixteen. The age difference didn't make any difference. "Me too," I said. "They look like the same girl to me, too."

There was no alteration in Mama's expression, no indication of surprise. "We'll examine them in the daylight, with a magnifying glass," she said. "If we can't see any differences, we'll talk to Sidney. He'll get an expert to examine them."

I got up and began washing our cups and saucers. I put the last cup in the dish rack when a thought occurred to me. I glanced toward Mama, whose face was set in determination. "If what you're saying is true, I don't know how we're going to prove it," I said.

Mama seemed puzzled by the thought, and then her gaze shifted. Her face softened into a smile. "Me neither," she said.

I felt almost overwhelmed. Nothing made sense. Two girls with different mothers and fathers couldn't look that much alike. "Suppose Chloe Ashley and Sara Turner *are the same*," I asked.

Mama hesitated, her look was frank. "We're back to square one."

CHAPTER SIXTEEN

I couldn't believe how my father looked when he walked into the kitchen. His caramel complexion had lost its glossy brown look. The lines in his face suggested a paper fold; his eyes were dark and weary.

When we got in from Benford, we assumed that he was in his bed, asleep for hours. Now he stood before us, fully dressed in jeans, a black leather jacket, black gloves and a black cap that covered a mix of gray and white hair. He took off his gloves, walked over to Mama and put his hands on her shoulders. "Hester is in the hospital," he said, his tone mildly apologetic.

There was a moment of startled silence. Mama's eyes searched his face. "What's wrong?" she asked.

"Nausea, vomiting, diarrhea, stomach cramps."

"Something she ate?"

"She tried to kill herself."

I held myself motionless and looked at the clock. It was 1:30 a.m. For a moment my mind was blank until the word suicide pushed through, a word that made me feel a bit disconnected.

Suicide isn't a part of our heritage, a part of our culture. There have been too many trials, too many disappointments, too many frustrations. We're a hopeful people. Things get bad, but we believe that life is precious, it's to be endured. What Hester had tried to do would bring mixed emotions to our family, our friends, our neighbors. I felt a combination of anger and pity, anger for what is considered cowardliness, pity for the misery she could no longer endure.

Mama stirred. "I'll go ."

"No," Daddy interrupted. "Tomorrow morning we'll go to the hospital together."

I was awakened in the wee hours with a telegram from my subconscious. "Pictures," the message said. My eyes came open and I stared. I sat up in bed, pushed the covers back, and flipped on the light, wincing at the sudden glare.

In my bare feet, I walked to the kitchen and looked for the pictures. They were still on the table. I sat, my elbows propped on the table, my chin in my hands. The girls looked identical.

What really bothered me was that I couldn't find a link between Mama's theory of Chloe impersonating Sarah and my vision of a man,the one that Chloe had ignited when I hit her with my car. What was I looking for? I thought idly about Martha's death, letting my mind wander. How surprised Chloe and Homeboy must have been when Martha told them I'd been to see her, had told them that I was looking for Chloe. It must have been a shock when he noticed my business card . I was with the Jacoby law firm. In his mind, somebody associated with the law could be dangerous. I considered what they thought about the announcement in the paper, wondered if it shook them up even more.

How would we find them, I wandered? There was a clue that tugged at me, something that linked me and that girl together, something that would lead me to them, some elusive piece of information, some interpretation of facts, something .

When I heard my father's voice, I jumped, my heart racing toward a heart attack. "Are you going to the hospital with us?" he asked, his tone matter-of-fact.

I took a deep breath, then let it out. "I don't think so," I stuttered. "I can't do anything there."

"Candi may need you," he said.

"I'll be here at the house," I whispered. "If she needs me, call."

Daddy's expression seemed to darken. "What's the matter with you?" he asked.

I laughed. "What makes you think something is wrong?"

"You've got a certain look," he said. "A kind of skittish expression, like you're trying to hide something."

"You misread me," I said.

He shook his head. "I don't think so," he said. "You do your nose a certain way when you're trying to be devious. You can't help it."

I smiled. "I'm fine," I said. "Kind of upset about Hester, that's all."

He poured a cup of coffee and sat next to me.

"I'm disappointed," he said. "I expected better from Hester," .

"She has been depressed since Fingers died," I said.

"That's no reason for her to try to kill herself"

Just about that time Mama walked into the kitchen, dressed in a pair of black slacks, a white and green sweater. I glanced at the wall clock. It was 6:30 a.m., too early for a hospital visit. "What about Bozie Jackson?" she asked.

Daddy frowned. "I was just about to tell Simone that the ambulance brought Bozie to the hospital about the same time as I got Hester there. He's had a heart attack ... looked like he was in bad shape," he said.

Mama shook her head. "We'd better get to the hospital," she said.

"It's too early," I said.

"I want to be there when the doctor visits," she said. "That's usually between 7:00 and 7:30."

Half an hour later, I was alone again. Cliff, who was asleep in the guest room, wouldn't be up for another couple of hours.

I ate a bowl of cereal, then poured myself a fresh cup of coffee. Something was nagging at me, and it had nothing to do with Hester or Bozie Jackson. It was the pictures. Something about them had set up a low hum in my mind that wouldn't stop buzzing.

I grabbed the two photographs again and studied them more carefully. The broad forehead, arched brows, high cheek bones and flat nose were the same. Sarah Turner's lips looked somewhat thinner. Then I heard myself make a startled sound ... not a real word, but something punctuated with an audible exclamation point. A small pendant the size of a locket hung around Chloe Ashley's throat. I searched for a magnifying glass to examine it.

Excitement bubbled up. Could Mama be right? Chloe and Sarah Turner might be the same girl. I waited an hour, then picked up the phone and called Clyde Collier. "Sorry to call so early," I said.

"It's.barely nine o'clock," he said, sounding as if he had just awakened.

"I know." I paused, feeling awkward. "I've been looking at the picture of your daughter and if you don't mind ..."

"What?"

I hesitated, debating. "Is there any way that you can stop your daughter from getting the money you mentioned?" I asked, keeping my tone flat, as matter-of-fact as I could make it.

"Why would I want to do that?"

"For her own protection."

"Who does Sarah need to be protected from?"

I sighed. This wasn't going to be as easy as I thought it would be. "I guess I'm thinking that since you've only seen Sarah once, it might be a good idea if you met with her personally before she got the money."

"It's too late for that. Over the past five years I've turned everything over to my Sarah."

"But you said she hadn't visited."

"Only through the mail," he said. "I've given her everything, power of attorney, everything through the mail."

I was surprised. "She'll get the trust and what-ever money you leave, too?"

"Sarah's my heir," he said. "You do understand. It's the right thing to do, and I'm for doing what's right."

I was confused. "I need some answers to a few questions. Please help me."

There was a silence.

"Do you have her address?"

"Just a minute."

I waited.

"Why are you so anxious to find my Sarah?" he asked when he'd returned.

I took a deep breath and thought about it for a moment. "I'm not sure that the young lady you've been communicating with over the past five years is your daughter Sarah."

He laughed at my tone. "If she's not my Sarah, then who is she?"

"I don't know," I interrupted. "But if we can talk to Sarah, I'll feel better!"

I could hear him breathe heavily. "The address is _____ _____," he said. "When you talk with Sarah, tell her to call me."

I agreed, then hung the phone on its cradle. I picked up the photographs again. These two girls looked alike, but they might not be the same. I had what I needed, an address, a starting point. When I returned to Atlanta, I would track down both girls from the moment they were born until one of them died, five years ago.

The phone rang.

"Simone," Mama said, her voice low, calm.

"Yes."

"Hester died a few minutes ago," she said.

"I'll come ."

"No," she said. "There's nothing to be done here. I'm coming home."

There was a silence.

"By the way," she said. "Bozie Jackson is dead, too."

"His heart?"

"He and Hester died within seconds of each other," she replied.

CHAPTER SEVENTEEN

I couldn't mourn for Hester. Cliff and I had driven to Hester's funeral in my car. I'd intended to skip the family gathering that always followed the death of one of its members. Family, friends and neighbors would be converging on Hester's house, but Cliff and I would go back to Otis, back to Mama's house. I needed to think and to plan how we were going to find Chloe or Sarah.

An hour after the funeral, we were feeling a very cold air at the grave side. The wind had picked up and a freezing breeze rattled the dead limbs in the nearby trees. We quietly left the crowd and drove away.

I was thinking how I'd always believed Hester to be spiritual and how her spirituality seemed to have failed her when Fingers died when the word *soap* intruded my thoughts. I heard myself whisper, "as far back as I can remember, Hester's made homemade soap!"

Cliff glanced at me.

The first thing I saw in my mind was Hester making soap. The next, the smell of lye and then the man's face. This time the vision went further .

I was in Hester's back yard; the man was sitting in a straight-back chair. The man was talking with Hester and she was laughing at what he said. There was a black wash pot with firewood underneath it. Chunks of pork fat were laying on a nearby table. A red can that had a picture of the devil on it with the an "X" nearby. Hester turned and warned me not to touch the can; if I did, I would die! The images were so vivid I stopped breathing.

Cliff seemed to know that something was wrong. He eased his foot on the brakes and slowed the car. "What's the matter?" he asked.

I raised my hand and closed my eyes trying to hide my anguish. The vision held on, dragging me back to a time where there were trees, a small vegetable garden, and a house. The house was situated near the trees, not far from a pond, or a lake. I put my hands over my mouth, trying to keep from making a sound.

For several minutes I said nothing. When I finally spoke, I was as surprised as Cliff of what I said. "Daddy told me that if he hadn't gone to Hester to buy soap, he'd never have found her laying on her kitchen floor!"

Cliff stared at me, his expression tinged with uncertainty. "What does that have to do with what's going on in your head?" he asked.

I waved for Cliff to pull to the side of the road. There was silence.

I rolled down my car window and took a deep breath; I felt exhausted. After a few minutes, the feeling began fading. I didn't know what to say, didn't know how to explain to Cliff or myself what was happening to me. "I think maybe that strange odor I smelled when I hit Chloe was lye, from cooked soap." I said.

Cliff said nothing. He was concentrating on my face, waiting for me to explain what I didn't even understand.

I broke eye contact. "Hester made soap. Lye soap."

Cliff was staring at me, a slight frown on his face. "Simone!" he shouted.

I nodded, realizing that I had to try to explain what I'd just gone through. "Okay, okay," I said. "The reason that I'm stuck on soap is that I thought I smelled something strange that I couldn't identify the day I hit Chloe. Now I know, it was lye soap that I smelled!"

Cliff leaned forward, a look of annoyance still on his face.

I turned toward the window and began rubbing my hands together. I was confused. I couldn't understand the connection between the girl, lye soap and Mama's cousin Hester.

Cliff waited.

Cliff leaned a little closer. He was silent for thirty seconds, which seemed like a long time. Reluctantly, he said, "It's hard to believe that your remembering the smell of lye soap on the girl is what caused you to become so upset."

I cut in. "It's true."

Cliff lifted one shoulder and scratched his head and stared at me. "Why would that cause you to look like you're about to jump out of your skin?"

I turned to look into his eyes. "Because I didn't understand that smell," I said.

"The soap smell may be a clue ..."

I interrupted. "Chloe or Sarah, whoever she is, could have gotten their soap from Hester and ..."

Cliff cut in. "Simone, they could have gotten their soap from anybody in Otis County who makes home made soap!" he said, a touch of irritation in his tone.

My heart began thumping. I was on the right track and nothing Cliff could say would change my mind. "Let's go to Hester's house," I said, knowing that the house where Hester had died wasn't the house I'd seen in my vision.

Cliff checked his watch. "It's a long shot if you think you'll find something in Hester's house that will lead you to Chloe!"

I glanced at the side view mirror as if another car was behind us. "I want to look through some of Hester's things," I said.

Cliff shook his head. "I'll be glad when you get that girl off your brain," he snapped. He turned the key in the ignition, put the car in gear, then eased forward on the shoulder until he could pull onto the pavement.

By the time we got to Hester's house, there was a crowd. The smell of mahogany-brown fried chicken, macaroni and cheese, collard greens, okra, field peas, rice, and a multitude of other items filled the kitchen and sashayed throughout the house. After a decent interval, no one seemed to pay any attention to me when I walked down the hall. They were too busy enjoying the feast.

Once inside Hester's bedroom, I locked the door behind me. I took a quick look at my surroundings. The room was the larger of two bedrooms, a space dominated by a king-sized bed and a big color television set. There were lots of clean white space, a gray carpet in an expensive wool shag. Three framed photographs of Fingers, a look of innocence in his dark eyes, were sitting on a white chest of drawers that matched the bed.

There was something incomplete, eerie and personal about this room. My imagination played out Hester's final morning. I could see her exhaustedly rolling out of bed, putting on her clothes, maybe combing her hair. Her spirit was low, she didn't want to eat, she felt anxiety, and probably hadn't slept much the night before. Whatever her normal routine, it had vanished when Fingers died. She had fallen into a bottomless pit and nothing would pull her up. I wondered whether Hester realized in those last fleeting moments of her life that Fingers might not have been worth the agony.

I walked to one of the windows and opened it, letting in some cold air. I took a very deep breath. The cold wind blew the pile of mail on top of her bedside table. I flipped through the envelopes and found a faded newspaper clipping that showed a picture of Fingers. The caption described how the boy had been shot and killed while trying to rob a nearby neighbor, Bozie Jackson.

I glanced at the clock. It was 4:00 p.m. when I found Hester's handwritten suicide note. Now, like a flood, the pity came. A lump rose in my throat. Hester's life and death had been tied up in what Mama described as the maternal instinct, the feeling that perpetuated life. The whole thing seemed stupid--dying because another person couldn't live. It made my stomach hurt!

I straightened the envelopes, putting the note on the top of the pile, then began looking through the top drawer of the night stand. I was shoving letters, envelopes, receipts, coupons and junk mail into a pile when a knock on the door startled me.

I hesitated, then unlocked the door.

Cliff peeked inside. "Mind if I come in?" he asked.

I nodded and stepped back. He strode into the room, a mischievous look in his eyes. "Find anything yet?" His voice was soft, low.

I avoided his gaze but pointed to the suicide note.

He read it, his expression changing to look as if he was fearful of the words that Hester had written shortly before she poisoned herself.

He put the note back on top of the envelopes, then stared at me for a few seconds. "Anything else?" he asked.

I looked at him hard, then shook my head. So many emotions were surging inside me that I felt a kind of dizziness.

He walked to the window, his hands in his pockets. He stared out, mumbling to himself. Then he walked around the room until he faced the closet. "I'll check in here," he said as he opened its door.

I turned toward the large chest of drawers and opened the top one. The drawer was a mess of underwear, bras, slips, and nightgowns. I picked up each piece and folded it until I had neat stacks, as if Hester needed to have me organize her personals.

I was about to think the whole thing stupid when I glanced at a small faded picture.

Cliff stepped out of the closet. "Nothing in there," he said.

I was sitting on the edge of the bed, my eyes frozen on the small photo. Memories flooded my mind and choked in my throat. I had found him! I had finally opened a door I recognized. I was beginning to remember.

Cliff crossed the room toward me. "What did you find?" he asked.

I thought I was prepared to deal with this, but I wasn't. My heart was beating so hard I could feel it through my blouse, a combination of excitement from my discovery and the stress of reliving a terrifying experience. The man's eyes, dark and deep set under heavy brows, stared at me in accusation. I handed the black-and-white picture, with its ominous dark splotches, to Cliff. He frowned as he examined the man and noticeably younger woman who sat in a back yard, a small lake faintly visible in the background. The man was in his forties, very thin. He wore a pair of black pants and a black shirt.

Cliff looked down at me for a few moments and said quietly, "This looks like Hester."

I blinked, then shifted in my seat. "It is Hester,"

I murmured.

"Who is the man?" he asked.

I looked at him for a long time before I answered. I felt breathless, a mixture of dread and guilt. "I don't know," I lied.

CHAPTER EIGHTEEN

I slept badly that night and spent Sunday morning trying to pull together the long forgotten details of a lost memory.

It was almost 1:00. We were in the kitchen, the one room in the house that seemed to get all the sunlight. Mama, wore a blue smock used only when she made bread, was up to her elbows in whole wheat flour. Pellets of dough clung to her fingers like wood putty. I turned in my chair as I explained the smell of lye soap on Chloe. Mama moved toward me when I pulled out the picture that I'd found in Hester's bedroom. She stood at the table, directly above my shoulders. "That's Kline Sapp, Hester's husband," she said, looking down at the photo.

"Fingers' father?" I asked.

Mama shook her head. "Fingers' father was killed in a logging accident. He didn't come into Hester's life until years after she had separated from that no-good Kline."

"Why do you say he was no good?" I asked.

Mama made a face ... distaste or dislike with a touch of anger. "He was mean, man, spiteful."

Daddy interrupted, as he poured himself a cup of coffee. "He used to beat Hester three times a day, for breakfast, lunch and supper!" he said.

I shifted uncomfortably as he added two spoons full of sugar and a sprint of milk into his coffee.

Mama gave me a direct look, the blacks and whites of her oval eyes pure and separate. "Hester was a good twenty years younger than Kline. He was so jealous, she couldn't even talk to her own cousins without him accusing her of sleeping with one of them. The last time he beat up on Hester, she was in the hospital for two whole weeks. Abe went after him to lock him up. He ran, and we ain't heard from him since!"

Daddy, who now leaned against the counter, shook his head with a kind of mock disgust. "I reckon he's dead by now. 'Course, people like Kline are too mean to die!" he said.

"He ain't dead," Mama said, as she returned to her dough. "Somebody told me they saw him in Ridgeland a few months ago."

"He wasn't at Hester's funeral," Daddy said.

Mama gestured dismissingly. "I never expected him to be," she said. "Knowing Kline, he's probably celebrating poor Hester's passing."

Cliff walked over to the refrigerator and took out two diet colas, which he brought back to the table. He popped both tops and passed one to me.

"I hate to say this but there's some connection between the girl we're looking for and Kline, Hester's husband," I said.

For a moment, nobody said anything as the news sank in.

Daddy moved away from the counter and walked to the table. "How do you know that?" he asked.

I took a deep breath and struggled with a resistance to share what finally made sense to me. I could see now that there had been a certain pleasure in not having to relate my experience to anyone. I bit back the impulse, passed the picture around the table and said, "I saw him through her!"

"Through her?" Cliff asked.

"Something about the girl's smell brought back the memory of Kline's' face," I said, feeling a sudden shift in my perspective and anxious not to sound like I'd had some kind of mystical experience.

They looked at me.

I tried to smile but from the expression on their faces, it must have looked more like I made a face. I was nervous, uncomfortable. "I didn't say anything earlier because I couldn't figure out what was wrong with me and I didn't understand the smell or..." I hesitated. "I felt like I'd been stuck. The whole thing wasn't real. I saw a face, like a face in a dream, familiar but unrecognizable. The harder I tried to remember where I'd seen it, the impression faded. The whole thing made me sick!"

Mama turned around and looked at me with a sort of curiosity. Then she smiled and passed the picture back to me. "How do you feel now?" she asked in a voice that always invoked a special chemistry between the two of us.

"I remember everything!" I said, feeling like I'd been nearsighted and had suddenly gotten glasses so that I could see things clearer. "This morning as I drank coffee and studied the picture, the scenes came together like a movie."

My family said nothing. They sat, studying me, their mental gears ready to go to work.

I took a deep breath and started telling my story, hoping that somehow in the telling I'd get rid of my protective feelings, or whatever it was that made me reluctant to share the incident.

"I remember I was a little girl sitting alone," I began. "My brothers said I was too young to play their games. There were large trees that stood above me blocking out the sun. There was the smell of roses mixed with the odor of lye from a big black wash pot.

"Three kittens, one black and the others black and white like my favorite dress, romped nearby. Red and blue birds bickered among the branches. They made me laugh.

"Then the wind changed. I smelled a different odor; it was the smell of Lysol. The smell gave me a funny feeling, like something scary was nearby. I looked up. A man's eyes were fixed on me. He wasn't a stranger, but he scared me. He said something, words I didn't understand.

"He reached for me but I moved away, my steps slow, uncertain. His eyes shifted, he growled. A single word slipped from his lips. I moved again because he made me feel like something was not right.

"Somewhere in the woods behind the house a

dog barked. I had the urge to run in that direction, so I broke out in a trot, stopping to see if the man had gone. He was behind me, taking giant steps in my direction. I turned and ran along a narrow path grown up with bushes. He was coming after me, I could hear him. He sounded like an animal, a bear. I ran as fast as I could, stopping every now and then to look back. The man was still behind me!

"I kept running, trying to put distance between us. The more I pressed, the closer he came. Finally, I couldn't run anymore. In front of me was a big pond, or maybe a lake. I dropped to the ground, struggling to breathe. A lump rose in my throat.

"His shadowy form eased towards me, a smile curled his lips. Sweat was pouring from his forehead; his scent was all over me. I wanted to throw up. My skin tingled, a chill spread through me.

"I started to cry. He put his hands around my neck and shoved me into the grass. The man's face tightened, his head twisted against his shoulder. 'I'm going to kill you, little girl!' he whispered, his voice cold.

"Suddenly, there was a rustling in the bushes, the sound of boys and a dog. The man stopped to listen, only his eyes moved.

"'*DON'T KILL ME!*' I choked.

"The man froze, his body rigid. His hands were still around my neck. His odor was pungent, the scent of Lysol burned in my mind, etched so deeply that I could never wipe it out.

"'Simone, is that you?' Will's voice shouted.

"The man's eyes, like arrows, glared at me, warning me not to speak. Slowly, his hands slackened; he stood above me, soundless, his eyes narrowed to slits.

"'Simone,' my brother hollered again. 'You better not be out here by yourself. If you are, you're going to get a whipping!'

"This time, Will's voice broke the spell; instinct told me what to do. My legs were up, I was leaping past the man, through a path in the woods. When I stopped running, my heart was pounding, my breath came in gasps, but I was safe . I was back in the house hiding under my bed!"

Mama's eyes held a maternal guilt that I'd never seen before. It nearly broke my heart. "You were five years old," she whispered. *"Only five years old!"*

I leaned back in my chair.

She continued. "I had to have my gallbladder removed. James was overseas. I asked Hester to keep you and the boys for the summer. It was the only time you were ever away from me. The only time!"

"It's okay. Kline didn't hurt me," I said. "If he had, I would have remembered that, too!"

Daddy was mad. "But he would have," he shouted. "That crazy Kline is just that mean!"

The expression on Cliff's face was a soft, gentle bewilderment. "Simone, I'm so sorry," he said, "so very sorry!"

I tried to smile. "When I looked into that girl's eyes and saw her fear, smelled the lye and saw the vision of the man's face, it threw me for a loop.

At first, I thought my eyes were playing tricks on me, then the visions began coming voluntarily, when I was away from the girl. I didn't know what to think!"

"I knew something was going on inside your head," Cliff said. "I only wish you'd said something!"

"How could I explain something that didn't make sense to me?"

"It makes sense now!" Mama said, her kneading completed and her hands washed. She was standing behind me, her hands resting softly on my shoulders. "The house, the pond is on the road past Riverside Baptist Church. Hester and Kline lived there when they first got married." I looked up into her eyes and saw that nothing would stop her from finding Kline Sapp or Chloe.

Daddy's eyes held a generous dose of irritation. His expression told me that on this one he was in total agreement with his wife. "When I get my hands on Kline," he said, "he'll be dead meat ."

I cut in. "It won't help to hurt him," I said, trying to dilute his anger. "It would be better if we could stop Kline, Chloe and whoever is with them from pulling off their fraud!"

Cliff cleared his throat and nodded. "It was such a shock for you. If we do manage to stop them, would that get rid of your fear? The guilt?" he whispered.

"No," I admitted.

Everybody stared at me again.

I felt adamant. "I've got to meet Kline Sapp face to face to show him that I'm not scared of him anymore!"

Daddy let his body sag and rolled his neck back and forth, as if he was trying to ease tension. Finally, he shook his head, his eyes straying toward the picture. "Like I said before, Kline Sapp is dead meat!"

I turned my head slightly, my gaze shifting to my father's face. "Kline Sapp and Chloe are trying to get a trust fund that doesn't belong to them. If we can catch them and prove it, the law will take care of whatever vengeance you need!"

Cliff picked up the picture of Hester and Kline. He shook his head and cleared his throat. "I don't know," he said. "It's going to be hard to find Kline, the girl and her boyfriend, too."

Mama took the photo from his hand. "I've got a plan that will net Kline, the girl and whoever else is in this mess with them!"

CHAPTER NINETEEN

Mama went about setting a trap. The first thing she did was to phone Clyde Collier to get him to agree to have his death announced in local newspapers in the surrounding counties.

The next week Cliff would solicit Mr. Collier's heirs and creditors. A telephone number would be given. We'd used the same operator as we'd used earlier because she knew how to get information before calling Cliff.

Would the man I'd named Homeboy and Kline Sapp come with Chloe to claim the money? We didn't know. We figured Chloe had tried to escape earlier and the men wouldn't take too kindly to letting her out of their sight when they were about to get their hands on the loot. We had to hope and wait.

Catching the trio was one thing; proving that they were crooks was another. We had nothing to confirm that they'd murdered Sarah Turner or Martha Benton.

I talked it over with Sidney. The most we could hope for was to prove that the three had intended fraud to get Sarah's inheritance.

The address Mr. Collier had given me was useful. All its mail was forwarded to a post office box in Otis County. I was glad because this got Sheriff Abe involved.

An order to exhume Chloe Ashley's body couldn't be obtained until we proved probable cause, but the sheriff got in touch with the coroner and set things up.

I spent the next few weeks doing my thing, running a paper trace on the girls. As Mama had suggested, Sarah and Chloe had met in school. They were both girls of mixed blood, both about the same age. Sarah had an anonymous benefactor, but Chloe's father was a man of modest means, a white man named David Ashley who was determined to educate his racially-mixed daughter.

The girls were involved in sports, the kind that required physical examination, so school records showed distinguishing features, birth marks.

A couple of teachers wrote about the mannerisms of both girls and, all in all, I got enough information to tell us whether or not it was Chloe or Sarah who had been buried. If not, dental and doctor records could be subpoenaed.

One month to the day, the call we wanted came. Sarah Turner told our operator she had read in the newspaper that her father had died. She wanted to claim his estate.

Cliff's legal manner served our cause well. When he talked to her over the phone, he went through a lot of jargon, mentioning papers of verification. After a few minutes, she agreed to meet him in Bedford at the home of her late father.

The day that everything went down was a contradiction. The weather was beautiful. A sunny day, temperature 69, a very slight breeze, with all the signs of spring.

Inside, my parents and I sat in a large bedroom across from the den in Clyde Collier's house. We looked like we were bears hibernating for the winter.

The room was at an angle that, when the door was slightly cracked and a mirror was placed strategically near the table where Cliff sat, we could see whoever sat in front of him from the waist upward. Cliff and my father had worked out this surveillance. It was the kind of thing that you'd expect to see in a movie; the whole thing seemed so unreal.

When the front doorbell rang, my heart took a jump. Cliff answered the door, his voice so low I could barely hear him. The other voices weren't so indistinct ... two men and a woman.

When the trio followed Cliff into the room, everything was confirmed. The girl, Chloe, wore jeans, a long-sleeved flannel shirt, and black boots. Both men wore long coats and large hats that almost covered their faces.

At first Chloe did the talking. Cliff asked a few questions such as her mother's name, the school she'd attended, the first meeting she'd had with Clyde Collier. Chloe's answers were short and to the point. When Cliff asked for identification, she pulled out papers and handed them over to him. It was then that she broke off eye contact.

The three people sat, avoiding eye contact with

each other, as Cliff read through papers.

I swallowed.

Cliff repeated a question and Kline Sapp gestured his irritation, showing the first signs of impatience. "She done proved that she's the dead man's daughter, what more do you want?" he asked.

Cliff apologized, then pulled out an official looking paper. He wanted to get Chloe's signature so that we could compare hers to the dead Sarah's. Chloe took a deep breath and started to sign the paper. Then, without looking at the men who had accompanied her, she hesitated.

Homeboy snapped. "Go on!"

Chloe didn't move.

"What's wrong with you?" Kline asked, an expression of uncertainty on his face.

The girl sat, her hands to her side.

"Is there something you don't understand?" Cliff asked. "Something I didn't explain?"

Chloe looked at Cliff, avoiding the other's gaze. She shook her head. "No, it's just that I've got to use the bathroom," she said.

"After you sign these here papers!" Homeboy snapped.

I could see Chloe's face; her expression was tinged with guilt.

"She can't go through with it," Mama whispered. "I can tell!"

"Now what?" I asked. "If she doesn't sign those papers, Abe can't hold them," I said.

My father shook his head. "When I finish with Kline, Abe won't have nothing to hold!" he said.

Chloe got up, crossed the room and went inside the door that Cliff pointed out as the bathroom.

"She'll probably try to escape again," Mama said.

"Now what?" I asked.

"We'll have to help her get away," Mama said.

Daddy's anger was mixed with confusion.

A few minutes later, Chloe was back in the room. She stood in front of Cliff and shook her head emphatically. "I'm not going to sign those papers," she whispered.

Homeboy jumped to his feet, grabbed her by the shoulders and looked into her eyes. "You're going to sign," he said, his voice as brutal as it had sounded when he had called me.

Chloe's movements were listless and haggard. She choked back tears. I figured she had gone into the bathroom to try to pull herself together.

When Kline stood up and walked over to Homeboy, my father couldn't hold off any longer. He burst out of the bedroom, my mother and I following close behind.

"What's going on?" Kline asked. He had barely gotten the words out of his mouth when my father punched him in the face.

Homeboy slipped a switchblade from his coat and grabbed Chloe around the throat. The poor girl shook her head as if to shut out the truth she could see written on his face.

Daddy started to ignore Homeboy and hit Kline again, but I screamed. My voice stopped his fist in mid air.

Mama started talking in her most hypnotic

voice. "Now, let's not panic," she said. "There is no reason for anybody to get hurt."

Homeboy's eyes grew wide. "What's this all about?" he asked.

"This has gotten out of hand," Cliff said, moving from behind the desk toward Homeboy.

Kline jerked forward, then shouted recognition, "James, Candi!"

Daddy looked at his fist, then shook his head. "You tried to hurt my little girl," he said. "You tried to kill Simone!"

Kline Sapp stared at me, then looked away. He was indeed a sick man...a man full of quarter-sized ulcers on his face and neck. The stench of his sickness filled my nostrils. Still, neither his odor nor his eyes were menacing to me anymore; this confrontation destroyed whatever monster I'd imagined this man to be.

Chloe stirred, her eyes widening as if she understood what was happening. Kline's recognition confused Homeboy even more. A few seconds later, he made the connection, and when he did, he took his hands from Chloe's throat and shoved her down into a chair.

Then he turned, our eyes locking. "You didn't take my hint," he said. "You're just like most black women, hard headed!"

A long silence, a terrible silence filled the room. My hands shook. "We know that this girl is Chloe Ashley and not Sarah Turner," I said, controlling the tremor in my voice.

Chloe stared at me, the color in her light skin draining from her face.

"You can't prove that," Homeboy said.

As I studied him, I remembered my vow to be a woman who would fight her enemies. "I've got proof. In my purse there are birth and death certificates."

"You ain't got a death certificate for Sarah Turner," he said.

"I've got something just as good," I said, reaching for my pocketbook.

My movement scared him . he rushed toward me with the open knife. Cliff dashed between us and hit him.

Homeboy dropped to the floor, then staggered to his feet, stumbling as he struggled to keep the knife in his hand. The wind had been knocked out of him; he gasped for breath. His fingers tightened around the knife. In the next second, he swung at Cliff who barely jumped out of his reach.

I looked around. My father had Kline on the floor, punching him in the face.

Mama, whose eyes threatened tears, took a step toward my father, then changed her mind. She tried to appear to be in charge, but I knew that neither of us had control. "For God's sake, James, stop it!" she shouted, her voice trembling.

Nausea wrenched my stomach. I saw that Cliff might get cut. I envisioned blood oozing out of his body. I took a deep breath. I took a deep breath and tried to keep my head clear. A tiny voice in the back of my head told me what to do . I pulled out my can of Mace and showered the room.

CHAPTER TWENTY

The six of us were in the kitchen of my parents : Mama, Daddy, Cliff, Sheriff Abe, and Chloe Ashley. We were having coffee, discussing how Mama had tracked and caught two thieves. And, of course, no doubt saved a victim.

Two weeks earlier, my parents, Cliff and I, along with Hank James (whom I'd named Homeboy), Kline Sapp and Chloe Ashley had to have Mace washed from our eyes at Benford Hospital. Later that same day, Hank James and Kline Sapp were arrested and charged with first-degree murder.

"Why did you agree to testify against that boyfriend of yours?" Daddy asked Chloe.

Mama looked at Chloe and smiled. It was a self-assured, in-total-control smile. then she nodded, encouraging Chloe to talk.

After a second, Chloe spoke through a slack smile. "When things first started," Chloe said, fingering a teaspoon, "I didn't see any harm in impersonating Sarah." She blinked nervously. "By the time I ran into Simone's car, I didn't want any part of Sarah's money, Hank or Kline Sapp!"

I leaned forward. "Did Homeboy take you from

the hospital against your will?" I asked.

Chloe turned to look at the sheriff, then she tilted her head toward me and nodded.

Mama put her coffee down on the table. "The straw that broke the camel's back," Mama interjected, "was when that crazy boy killed Martha Benton, wasn't it?"

"Hank did kill Martha?" Cliff asked.

Chloe nodded again. "Sarah and I visited our missing parent during that trip five years ago. We'd spent years talking about it and another year planning for the meeting. When I finally saw my poor mother, she was a broken woman. I had been her only child, a child born out of a rape by a white man she'd worked for. When I was born, looking more white than black, he took me from her and raised me by himself." She hesitated. "Oh, don't misunderstand me, he was good to me. But whenever I asked about my mother, he'd tell me to forget that I came from a woman. When I finally saw Martha, she was poor and black, but I loved her instantly!"

"That's why you kept phoning her over the years?" I asked.

Chloe sat back. "When I called Martha and she told me of your visit and gave me your phone number, I made the mistake of telling Hank."

"Homeboy?" I asked.

She frowned. "He was always after me to stop calling Martha. He wanted me to believe that I was no longer Chloe but Sarah, but I couldn't . I couldn't lose Martha after I'd spent a lifetime thinking of how it would be when I found her."

"So he killed her?" Cliff asked.

"Hank poured gasoline around Martha's house and set it on fire. Kline guarded me; I sat in the car and watched him do it. It was horrible!"

"My God!" Daddy began.

Tears began to stream down Chloe's face. "He always talked about getting rid of Martha." Chloe looked at me. "He tried to convince me that it was the only way to stop you from looking for me," she sobbed.

"He was almost right," I said, laying my hand gently on her forearm.

Sheriff Abe looked up. "With Chloe's testimony, we'll have Hank James for murder and Kline Sapp as his accomplice," he said.

"I never understood how Kline Sapp got involved in the whole thing," Cliff said.

Chloe wiped her eyes and I realized that she was indeed a pretty girl. "Hank and I started seeing each other a year before Sarah and I visited our parents," she said. "We were talking about getting married, so it was natural for me to tell him about our intended visit. Hank thought it was a good idea and he offered to drive us to South Carolina since he had a relative, an uncle, who lived nearby. That uncle was Kline Sapp."

I glanced down at my mug of coffee. "Whose idea was it for you and Sarah to switch identities?" I asked.

"Kline thought of it," Chloe said. "From the minute he saw both of us, he swore we looked alike. Over the years, other people had said we looked identical. Sometimes our teachers couldn't tell us apart.

"After the accident, Kline talked Hank into kidnapping Sarah from the hospital. He concocted the scheme that if she died, we'd bury her in my name and I'd take on her identity so that I could get her money, money Sarah had told us would be hers in five years.

"Kline knew that nobody around here had known either of us, and both Martha and Clyde Collier had only seen us that one time."

"You went along with the switch," I said.

"At first, I reasoned that Sarah would have wanted me to have the money."

Nobody said a word.

"As time went on, I began to feel that once they got their hands on Sarah's money, I'd become disposable. As a matter if fact one night, I overheard Kline say that after they got the money, I wouldn't be needed," Chloe said.

"They were going to kill you?" I said.

"Yeah," she said, then hesitated. "They must have gotten the idea that I suspected what they had in mind because they began to keep a close watch on me. They wouldn't let me out of their sight. At first, we stayed in a cabin near Oaktree, but about two months before the accident with Simone, they moved me to an old house down the road from Riverside Baptist Church."

"A house near a fish pond?" I asked uneasily.

Mama looked toward me, her eyes keen and alert. "Like I told you, it was the house that Kline and Hester stayed in when they were first married, the one they were staying in the summer you spent with them."

I swallowed.

"You were a long way from Riverside Church when Simone hit you," Daddy said from the refrigerator where he was extracting a container of orange juice.

"I caught a ride to Oaktree Crossing. The driver was headed to Eatonville, so I got out to try to get another ride down 601 into Otis."

"Where were you going?" Daddy asked.

"As far away from Hank and Kline Sapp as I could get," she said.

"It was the way you smelled that must have brought back my memories of Kline," I said.

"Kline taught Hester how to make the lye soap," Mama said.

Daddy leaned back in his chair. "Kline had better be glad that Abe's got him locked up," he said.

"Daddy, I told you, Kline didn't hurt me," I said.

"He would have. He's just mean enough to hurt a five-year-old girl!" Daddy said.

Mama's glance rested warmly on me. Her eyebrow lifted. "Thank God he didn't hurt you, Simone!"

I smiled. "You tracked him, you caught him, and you stopped him," I said. "Kline Sapp is history, a chapter in my life I can bury now!"

Cliff loaded his second cup of coffee with sugar. "As long as nobody soaks their feet in Lysol," he said, *"everything will be all right!"*

And, Mama smiled.

NORA DELOACH is a native of Orlando Florida, presently living in Georgia. She is married and the mother of three children. She began writing in 1991 and her first effort, *Silas*, was accepted on the first submission (to Holloway House). Her Candi and Simone Covington mystery series (***Mama Solves A Murder, Mama Traps A Killer, Mama Saves A Victim and this title, Mama Stands Accused***) followed.